**Gina had almost been killed.**

Shane ran a hand over the back of the truck's seat. Applying a little pressure on the backrest, he could feel the sharp tip of the arrow where it had gone through the metal of the truck. So close. He breathed out a prayer of thanksgiving.

Another inch and the arrow would have skewered Gina in the back.

Gina came out of the police station. "Tell me what's happening." She spotted the arrow sticking out of the back of the cab and gasped. "Do you think... Did my brother do this?"

Shane wouldn't sugarcoat the truth. "Unless there's someone with a vendetta against the K-9 trainers, which I doubt, I can't think of anyone else who wants you dead. Can you?"

She wrapped her arms around her middle. "No."

Shane didn't like her standing outside, making herself an easy target if her brother had followed them to the station. "Come on, let's get back inside."

Gina followed Shane into the station and sank onto a bench.

Bella, Shane's K-9 partner, went to her and put her chin on Gina's knees.

That told Shane a lot.

**Terri Reed**'s romance and romantic suspense novels have appeared on *Publishers Weekly* top twenty-five and Nielsen BookScan's top one hundred lists and have been featured in *USA TODAY, Christian Fiction Magazine* and *RT Book Reviews*. Her books have been finalists for the Romance Writers of America RITA® Award contest, the National Readers' Choice Award contest and three times in the American Christian Fiction Writers' Carol Award contest. Contact Terri at terrireed.com or PO Box 19555, Portland, OR 97224.

## Books by Terri Reed

### Love Inspired Suspense

#### Rookie K-9 Unit

*Protect and Serve*

#### Northern Border Patrol

*Danger at the Border*
*Joint Investigation*
*Murder Under the Mistletoe*
*Ransom*

#### Capitol K-9 Unit

*Duty Bound Guardian*

#### Protection Specialists

*The Innocent Witness*
*The Secret Heiress*
*The Doctor's Defender*
*The Cowboy Target*

Visit the Author Profile page at Harlequin.com.

# PROTECT AND SERVE

## TERRI REED

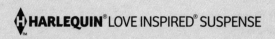

HARLEQUIN® LOVE INSPIRED® SUSPENSE

Special thanks and acknowledgment are given to Terri Reed
for her contribution to the Rookie K-9 Unit miniseries.

LOVE INSPIRED BOOKS

Recycling programs
for this product may
not exist in your area.

ISBN-13: 978-0-373-67743-6

Protect and Serve

www.Harlequin.com

**Printed in U.S.A.**

For God has not given us a spirit of fear,
but of power and of love and of a sound mind.
*−2 Timothy* 1:7

To my family and my critique partners
for your encouragement, love and support.
And to my editors Emily Rodmell and Tina James
for inviting me to write this book and for believing in me.
Thank you!

# ONE

"Georgiiiinnnaaa!"

Gina Perry froze midstride in the center of her bedroom. An explosion of panic detonated in her chest. She recognized the unmistakable singsong tone of her brother.

Oh, no. No, no, no. Tim had tracked her to Desert Valley, Arizona.

Frantic with alarm, she whirled around to search the confines of her upstairs bedroom. The sliding glass door to the terrace stood open, allowing the dark March night air to fill her house.

Where was he? How had he discovered where she'd been hiding? Had she made a fatal error that brought him to her door?

She stumbled backward on shaky legs just as her brother stepped from the shadows of her closet.

Light from the bedside table lamp glinted off the steel blade of a large knife held high in his hand. His face was covered by a thick beard, his hair stuck out in a wild frenzy and the mania gleaming in his hazel eyes slammed a fist of fear into her gut.

Choking with terror, she turned and fled down the stairs.

She couldn't let him catch her or he'd make good on his threat to kill her. Just as he had their father two years ago.

Her bare feet slid on the hardwood steps. She used the handrail to keep her balance.

Tim pounded down the stairs behind her, the sound hammering into her like nails on a coffin.

Her breathing came out in harsh rasps, filling her head with the maddening noise. She made a grab for her phone on the charger in the foyer but missed. Abandoning the device, she lurched for the front door and managed to get the lock undone and the door opened.

Without a backward glance, she sprinted into the night, across the small yard to the road. Rocks and debris bit into her bare feet, but she ignored the pain. *Faster!*

*Dear God, help me!*

The Desert Valley police station was only half a mile down the quiet residential road on the west side of town. Street lamps provided pools of light that threatened to expose her. She ducked behind the few cars parked along the curb and moved rapidly through the shadows.

She had to reach the police station. Only there would she would be safe.

There, Tim couldn't hurt her.

"Sisssster! I'm coming for you!"

He wasn't far behind. She'd never make it to the station before he caught her. But the K-9 training center where she worked was closer. If she could get inside, she could call for help.

Grateful the moon hid behind cloud cover on this spring night, she stayed in the shadows and prayed she'd make it to safety. Just a little farther now. Her lungs burned from exertion. Her heart pounded in her chest.

Not daring to glance back to see how close Tim had gained on her, she ran for the training center and dove behind the bushes growing along the fence of the small outdoor puppy-training yard. She sent up a silent plea to God above that Tim wouldn't find her in the bushes.

"You can't hide from me," Tim shouted, his voice taking on the manic tone she knew all too well. A tone that had always sent her into hiding when they were kids.

Her body trembled with fear. She curled into herself, hoping to make herself smaller, less of a target for him to spot. The unmistakable sound of his heavy breathing as he passed by her hiding place tormented her. She bit her lip, drawing blood, the coppery taste making her gag. She clamped a hand over her mouth.

"You betrayed me, Gina. For that you'll pay. I'm going to kill you as soon as I find you."

His voice sounded farther away now. He'd moved past the yard and was nearly at the end of the next building. She breathed a small sigh of relief. But she couldn't relax. She wasn't safe yet. She had to get inside the training center.

Cautiously, she made her way along the training yard fence in a low crouch. The gate to the yard was open. Odd. All the trainers were careful to keep them closed and locked in case a dog escaped from the center and made it outside. It was as much for the dogs' protection as the general public's.

She rounded the corner and froze.

Someone lay faceup on the ground, half in, half out of the gate.

Moving closer, Gina recognized Veronica Earnshaw.

Gina's boss.

Panic crawled up Gina's throat and she gasped for air.

There were two gaping wounds in Veronica's chest.

Oh, no. No! Had Tim done this? Had he come to the training center first and, when he'd failed to find Gina, hurt Veronica instead?

Gina scuttled closer. *Please, Lord, don't let her be dead.* "Veronica?"

With a trembling hand, she put two fingers against Veronica's neck.

No pulse. Gina's heart sank.

It seemed, once again, God had ignored Gina's

plea. Just as He had when Gina witnessed her brother murder their father.

She choked back a sob. Tears blurred her vision. It should have been her lying in the dirt, not Veronica.

A scrape of noise echoed in the stillness of the night. Her brother retracing his steps?

She scuttled back to the bushes, burrowing in deep and drawing her knees to her chest. A line of Scripture wove through the shock numbing her mind. She clung to it like a lifeline. *The Lord is with me, I will not be afraid.*

The litany echoed through her head, mocking her. Because she was afraid. Deathly afraid.

Officer Shane Weston and his canine partner, a German shepherd named Bella, walked along Desert Valley Road. The cool Arizona night air smelled of the fragrant western honey mesquite trees that had started to flower as spring arrived.

It was dark, nearly ten o'clock, but Shane couldn't remain cooped up inside the condo he was staying in, one for out-of-town trainees. He was restless, anxious to see where he'd be assigned. He'd put in a request for his hometown police department of Flagstaff, but no one could guarantee he'd get his choice or even that he had a choice.

This past Friday, he'd completed his twelve-week training session at the Canyon County Training

Center, a pilot project for the state of Arizona that trained new police recruits to be K-9 officers.

Not every candidate who applied was selected for the K-9 program. Shane had been thrilled that he'd made the cut. Once he was accepted, he'd been placed with a group of other rookies, and they'd attended the police academy together in Phoenix before coming to Desert Valley for the K-9 training.

Upon the start of every twelve-week session, the trainers matched each officer with a dog based on master trainer Veronica Earnshaw's research into the rookies, along with questionnaires the recruits filled out prior to the start of the program.

Shane had gleaned that all the trainers used their instincts and knowledge of dogs to help with the pairing of officers to canines. The center was a well-run operation, highly respected throughout the state and a model for other centers.

Shane couldn't be more pleased with his pairing to Bella.

He knew, however, that once the training began, if a dog and rookie officer hadn't jelled for whatever reason and the trainers' attempts to intervene failed, then the officer and dog were reassigned to work with new partners to finish out the program.

Thankfully, he and Bella had meshed from the moment they were introduced.

Now that training was complete, the officers and their canines would be allocated to various police stations throughout Arizona, and the training center would then be reimbursed by the police stations. A win-win for everyone.

Shane sent up another quick prayer that his request would be honored and he'd be assigned to the Flagstaff PD, where he could prove to his brothers and father that he wasn't weak. He wasn't a failure.

He planned to be the best officer he could be, with ambitions to one day make captain, or even chief. One day he'd be the one in charge, and then he'd finally earn his family's respect.

Shane waved a greeting to an older man taking out his trash.

Very few people were out on this Saturday night, and those who were made a point of acknowledging him and Bella. Shane liked that the community of Desert Valley embraced the K-9 officers and their canine partners. He couldn't say the same of bigger cities, where law enforcement was usually viewed with fear, suspicion and malice.

Bella stopped abruptly, her ears perking and her nose lifting to smell the air.

Unease tightened Shane's shoulder muscles. She'd been alerted to something. "What is it, girl?"

Bella took off. Keeping the beam of the flashlight aimed ahead of him, Shane ran to keep up, his feet pounding noisily on the pavement. The lead connected to the dog's collar pulled taut, and Shane pressed himself to move faster. They headed toward the training center. Had something happened to one of the dogs? The trainers?

Bella led him past the veterinary clinic and skidded to a halt at the outdoor puppy-training yard.

Shane stopped and kept Bella at his side. He swept his flashlight over the scene before him. Dread crimped his chest. He sucked in a quick breath.

Veronica Earnshaw lay twisted on the ground with her dark hair and striking face coated in dirt. Her open eyes stared at the stars above. And what appeared to be two gunshot wounds marred her chest. Bile rose in his throat.

His priority as the first officer on the scene was to determine if the victim was alive or dead.

Bella tugged at the leash. He gave her the hand movement to sit and stay. She obeyed, but her gaze was riveted to the bushes along the fence.

Was the perpetrator hiding in there?

Wishing he had his sidearm, which he'd left locked up in the condo, he shone the flashlight on the thick shrubbery. He let out Bella's lead. She made a beeline for the greenery and sat staring at the dense foliage.

Caution tripped down his spine. There was no coverage for him to use. If the person who'd shot Veronica was in the bushes with the gun, he might well be the next victim.

"I'm a police officer. If someone is in there, you better come out," he said with authority.

"Shane?"

He knew that voice. "Gina?" It was the junior

trainer from the Canyon County training facility. A sob came from the bushes, then Gina crawled out. He reached out to help her and she flinched. Her long auburn braid was coming undone. The hazel of her eyes was nearly gone because of her enlarged pupils.

He held up his hands, palms out.

Was Gina's shock real or fake? Had she committed murder? Or was she a witness?

Cautious, in case there was a gun he couldn't see, he crouched beside her, noting blood on her hands and smeared on her khaki pants and pink sweater. "Gina. Are you hurt?"

"No." She took a shuddering breath. "She's dead. Veronica's dead. He killed her."

A witness, then. He refocused his attention on Veronica. There was no discernible movement of the upper part of her abdomen, indicating her breathing had stopped or was too shallow to be observed.

He checked for a pulse and found none. He shone the flashlight into her eyes—no response.

There was no question in his mind.

Gina was correct.

Veronica Earnshaw was dead.

His chest tightened; his lungs seized. An itch scratched at his throat. He put his hand on the inhaler in his pocket, but he refused to let the asthma take hold. There were procedures to follow. A crime to investigate. He had no time for an asthma attack right now. And as the first responder, he had a responsibility to make sure no element of the scene was disturbed any worse than it had already been.

Instead of his inhaler, he took out his cell phone and called the police department. When the dispatcher answered the call, he said, "This is Officer Shane Weston. I need assistance at the side yard of the Canyon County Training Center. One gunshot-wound victim. One potential witness."

He hadn't ruled out perpetrator. Not yet.

"I'll let the chief and Officer Hayes know," she responded before the line disconnected.

Slipping his phone back into his pocket, he made mental notes of the scene since he didn't have a notepad and pen. When he left the condo, he hadn't expected to end up working a crime scene.

He hadn't heard the report of a gun, much less two shots, so he knew this tragedy hadn't happened recently. Unless…a noise suppressor had been used.

The thought stuck in his mind like a thorn.

Because if that were the case, then Veronica's murder was premeditated.

He did a quick visual search with the flashlight for the weapon but came up empty. A dark trail of what he assumed to be blood led from Veronica to the training center doors. Had Veronica been dragged out of the building or had she managed to crawl to the gate seeking help?

As he waited for the Desert Valley police, he turned his attention to the woman sitting on the ground by the bushes. She'd drawn her knees to her chest and had begun rocking. Compassion tangled with suspicion. As much as he didn't want to think ill of Gina, she certainly had a reason to dislike the lead trainer.

"Gina, can you tell me what happened?"

She didn't acknowledge him but kept rocking, her gaze locked on something only she could see. He gently touched her shoulder.

She started and scrambled away from him. "No, please, no," she cried and curled into a tight ball.

He backed away, giving her space. "Gina, I'm not here to hurt you."

She raised her teary gaze to meet his. She blinked as the glazed fog lifted. "Oh, Shane. We're not safe. He's here. He found me."

A knot in his chest tightened. He? "Who are you afraid of?"

A visible tremor ran over her. "My twin brother, Tim."

"Wait, you have a twin?" He'd had no idea.

"Yes. Two years ago he escaped police custody in Mesa and disappeared." She rubbed at her temples. "I moved to Desert Valley to hide from him. I had hoped he wouldn't find me here. But he has. And now…"

Concern arced through Shane. They had an escaped criminal on the loose. Gina's twin brother. Had he killed Veronica thinking he'd shot his sister? Or was this a contrived story to cover Gina's crime? Was there really a brother, much less a twin? He didn't know her well enough to know if she had a sibling. "What happened to Veronica?"

"I'm not sure. I found her like this. I checked for a pulse." She looked away. "There isn't one."

He winced. She'd already contaminated the scene—if she wasn't the perpetrator. "Don't touch anything else or move again until the chief arrives, okay?"

She nodded on a shuddering breath.

"Why do you think your brother killed Veronica?" Shane asked her.

"Isn't it obvious?" She stared up at him. "He came here looking for me and instead found Veronica. He killed her out of rage because I wasn't here."

"You didn't see it happen?" Though her explanation was plausible, there were holes. "How would he know where you work?"

"I don't know. He's smart."

"But you don't work here anymore, right?"

"What?" Her voice held a note of confusion.

"Didn't Veronica put you on indefinite probation?" It had been a spectacle. Veronica had turned her mean streak onto Gina yesterday right in front of the newest class of graduated rookies. Veronica had loudly and very publicly claimed Gina had used the wrong training technique and declared Gina was on probation indefinitely.

Shane had attempted to talk to Gina after the incident because he'd felt bad for the pretty trainer, but she'd hurried home and he hadn't seen her until now.

Gina's shoulder rose and fell. "She did. But in typical Veronica fashion, she called me this morning to apologize."

"That's surprising," he said. "She didn't strike me as someone who would own her mistakes easily."

One side of Gina's mouth curled. "Oh, it wasn't a humble gesture. She does this almost every session. She gets mad for some perceived infraction and makes a scene." Gina blew out a breath. "Veronica needed me to return to the center to process the intake of three new German shepherd puppies donated by Marian Foxcroft."

"So you were here today."

"Yes. This morning." She wiped her forearm across her forehead. "I would have been at the training center this evening if I hadn't already committed to serving at the community church's Saturday-night potluck dinner."

He hadn't known she attended church. He hadn't seen her there these past few Sundays. "Do you mean the church's singles' potluck?"

She nodded.

For some reason the idea of her mingling with other singles rubbed him wrong. Which was so out of left field and inappropriate at the moment. Irritated at himself, he pushed the thought aside to focus on Gina.

Fresh tears rolled down her cheeks. He hated seeing her cry. Yet there was a jaded part of him that wondered if the tears were real. Were they a ploy to gain his sympathy?

"Veronica wasn't pleased that I couldn't be here tonight," she said. "But she agreed to microchip the new puppies and expected me to take over their care and training first thing on Monday morning."

However, that didn't explain how Gina came to be here now. Something about her story felt off.

The sounds of Desert Valley Police Department's finest arriving drew Shane's attention. Since the station was so close, several officers came on foot while the chief of police and the lone K-9 officer of the department drove to the training center.

"Is that...?" Louise Donaldson, the first officer to reach the scene, clamped a hand over her mouth and turned away.

Officer Dennis Marlton put a hand on her back and bowed his head as if the sight were too much to bear.

Officer Ken Bucks staggered back several steps. Though it was too dark to see his expression, Shane imagined that seeing an acquaintance murdered like this must be a shock, to say the least.

The last murder victim in the community of Desert Valley had been the wife of K-9 officer Ryder Hayes five years ago. A murder that had never been solved.

Shane glanced at Ryder, his face hidden in shadows created by the many flashlight beams directed toward the victim. Sitting at Ryder's side was his canine partner, a handsome yellow Lab named Titus. Shane had seen the pair around but hadn't really had a reason to interact with the Desert Valley Police Department's only official K-9 officer.

Chief Earl Jones, a tall, imposing seventy-year-old man with thick graying hair, knelt beside Veronica and checked for a pulse, apparently to confirm Shane's pronouncement that the master trainer was dead.

When he lifted his head, tears shone in his gray eyes. He stood, his hands fisted at his side. He was clearly struggling to contain his grief and anger. "Who did this?"

"Gina believes her brother, Tim Perry, did," Shane said, noting that Gina hadn't moved, just as he'd instructed her. "She didn't see it happen, though. I haven't asked her how she came to be here tonight."

"Hmm, her brother, huh?" Earl scrubbed a hand over his jaw.

"Apparently he's a wanted criminal in Mesa," Shane added. Did the chief know Gina had a brother who was in trouble with the law? Or had she kept that information hidden? The thought made him wonder what else she could be hiding. Was Gina capable of murder? Was the story about her brother a convenient way to deflect blame?

# TWO

"All right, everyone." The chief's voice held a sharp edge that swept over the group outside the Canyon County Training Center's side yard. "We have a crime scene and a potential suspect. Let's work this for Veronica and bring her killer to justice." His voice broke on the last word.

Shane felt for the man. It was no secret that the chief and Veronica had had a special relationship. Though they weren't related, Chief Jones regarded Veronica as the daughter he'd never had.

And despite complaints from other trainers and rookies that she was too harsh, critical and demanding, Chief Jones's philosophy was if you couldn't handle working with Veronica, how could you handle all the stress of being a cop or training police dogs and their handlers?

Chief Jones barked out orders for Marlton to fetch standing lamps and Bucks to call the coroner and start documenting the scene. "Donaldson, gather forensic evidence."

Officer Marlton left and returned a few minutes later with two huge freestanding lamps. Within moments, pools of sharp glaring light replaced the darkness.

Shane and Bella stepped out of the way as Ryder and his dog moved past. Shane could only imagine Ryder was remembering his wife's murder. But in this case they had a clear suspect. They would solve Veronica's murder.

Chief Jones pinned Shane with a questioning look. "Have you cleared the building?"

"No, sir, I was waiting with Gina."

Earl turned to Ryder. "You good?"

Taking a deep breath, Ryder nodded. "Yes, sir."

"Clear the building," the chief instructed. "And, Ryder, be careful."

"Yes, sir." Ryder and Titus headed toward the training facility door, keeping a wide berth around the dark, bloody trail.

The chief ran a hand over his graying hair. "I'll need to let her brother, Lee, know. He's the only family she had left." He shook his head with sadness.

"Is he here in town?" Shane asked. He hadn't known Veronica had a brother.

"No, he's in the state prison. He was convicted of larceny a few years back."

Shane bit back his surprise as he turned his attention to Gina. Seemed she wasn't the only one with brother issues.

Officer Donaldson squatted down in front of Gina. "Honey, I need to swab your hands for gunpowder residue."

A stricken look crossed Gina's lovely face, making her already pale complexion even more so. "I didn't shoot her. I don't even know how to handle a gun."

"It's procedure," Officer Donaldson explained as she worked. "Our department isn't large enough to employ a crime scene technician, so all of us officers have been trained to do basic forensic collection." She bagged the pad that she'd swiped over Gina's hands and face.

"I touched Veronica to see if she—" Gina turned away.

"I'll send everything gathered to the lab in Flagstaff. As long as the particle count is twenty or less, then you're fine. Cross contamination happens."

"But even if you don't find any sign of gunpowder on Gina, the lack of forensic evidence could be explained away," Shane said. "Someone wearing gloves when they pulled the trigger wouldn't have any residue on their hands. There could be some blowback on the perpetrator's clothing."

Gina whipped her attention to him.

"True," Officer Donaldson said. "The lab won't be able to process Gina's clothes until she's able to surrender them."

The flash of a camera burned Shane's eyes. Officer Ken Bucks snapped shots of Veronica's body.

"Marlton," the chief called to the older officer standing off to the side, observing.

"Yeah, Chief," Dennis Marlton answered, but didn't step closer. He had his arms folded over his potbelly as if protecting his paunch. He was shorter than his coworkers and had gray, thin hair and watery blue eyes that squinted at the chief.

"You and…" Earl frowned as he glanced around. "Where's Harmon?"

Dennis shrugged. "Late as usual."

The chief harrumphed. "Bucks, go with Marlton to canvass the area. See if anyone saw anything that might be helpful."

Bucks looked at the chief, his face glowing a pasty white in the light of the lamps. "I'm taking photos." He pointed to the trail of blood. "You said to document everything before we lose any evidence."

"Right. Stay on it." Earl turned his sharp steely eyes back on Officer Marlton. "You can handle the interviews alone."

Officer Marlton sighed heavily and unfolded his arms. "Fine." He trudged off, mumbling about having to do everything himself.

Shane watched him. His father, a police chief in Flagstaff, would never have stood for such disrespectful behavior from his men. First Harmon not showing up, then Bucks defying an order and Marlton making it clear he wasn't happy doing his job.

There was a rumor going around that Chief Jones

would be retiring soon. Perhaps that was why the chief wasn't strict with his employees. Or it could be the grief and shock of Veronica's death.

"I've gathered what I can from Gina," Officer Donaldson remarked as she held on to the evidence bags.

"Thank you, Louise. We'll get Gina's clothes bagged. Would you track down Harmon and then start a search for Tim Perry? Build a profile. I want to know where he's been and what he's been doing."

Louise nodded, her usually serious expression even more grim on her pale face. "On it."

Earl squatted down in front of Gina. "When was the last time you saw your brother?"

Her hazel eyes looked too large for her petite face. "Do you mean before tonight?"

Shane frowned. "So you did see him tonight."

She kept her gaze on the chief. "When I returned home from the potluck, he was in my bedroom. He had a knife. I ran downstairs hoping to get to the phone but he was too close so I escaped out the front door and ran this way, hoping to make it to the station, but then I found…" She closed her eyes.

"Why were you hiding in the shrubs when Bella and I arrived?"

Her eyelids popped open. "I was afraid you were Tim."

Or was she hoping she could slip away undetected?

A car pulled up. Shane yanked his gaze from

Gina to see Sophie Williams, another trainer at the center, emerge from behind the wheel. Tall, earthy and willowy, the former K-9 cop's normally confident demeanor was lacking as she hurried over.

Her shoulder-length blond hair was tied back in a messy ponytail, and her hazel eyes were anxious as she took in the scene. She and Veronica had clashed many times during Shane's weeks of training. He watched Sophie closely. Was her shock real? Could she and Gina have come up with a plan to off their boss?

Sophie halted beside Shane, but her gaze was on Veronica. "Oh, no. Is she…?" She clamped a hand to her mouth. Tears leaked down her face.

"Sophie, what are you doing here?" Earl asked, clearly puzzled by her presence.

"I heard on the police radio that something had happened at the center," she explained. Her teary-eyed gaze moved to Gina and widened. "Oh, no, Gina. Are you all right? Were you attacked, too?"

Before Gina could answer, Earl filled Sophie in on the details. It was clear by the way his voice shook that he was hanging on to his composure by the tips of his fingers.

A few minutes later, Randolph Drummond, the mortician who doubled as the coroner, arrived wearing a subdued black suit, white button-down shirt and black tie. He carried a medical bag. He stopped a foot away from Veronica's body to don gloves and booties, then he squatted beside her.

Bella whined. Shane stroked her head. She let out a loud bark just as a commotion broke out near the doors. Two small German shepherd puppies raced out of the center, followed by Titus and Ryder. The older dog circled the puppies, unmistakably in an attempt to corral them.

"Oh, no," Sophie said.

Gina jumped to her feet. "The puppies are loose. How...?"

Shane snagged Gina by the elbow before she could chase after the puppies. "We need your clothes."

She blinked at him, then grimaced. "Of course."

Shane turned to the chief. "Veronica was micro-chipping the puppies tonight and was supposed to come over to the condo afterward to work with James and Hawk." K-9 rookie officer James Harrison and Shane shared the furnished condo used by out-of-town rookies. "I'll call James and let him know what's going on. Maybe Hawk will be helpful." James's bloodhound, Hawk, specialized in crime scene evidence.

The chief held up a hand. "Have him clear Gina's house before you take her home to change. Bring back her current clothing in an evidence bag."

"Sir," Shane spoke up. "Shouldn't she be taken to the station for questioning?"

Gina let out a small gasp. "You can't really believe that I..."

The stricken hurt in her eyes stabbed at him, but

he couldn't rule her out as the murderer, not until forensic evidence cleared her. "You had a very good reason to want to hurt Veronica."

"So did many other people," she shot back.

"True." Including the other trainer, Sophie. Could the two women have conspired to murder their boss? Though Sophie had once been a cop, that didn't mean she couldn't have colluded with Gina. Hmm. Something to talk to the chief about later.

To Gina, Shane said, "Veronica humiliated you on Friday. And from what I've heard, she stole the fiancé of one of your best friends." He hated throwing the rumor in her face but it went to motive.

"It's true Veronica did steal Simon from Jenna just to prove she could. It broke Jenna's heart and caused her to resign and leave, not only the training center but Desert Valley." Gina squared her shoulders. "And yes, I may have loathed my boss, but I never wished Veronica dead."

He wanted to believe her. There was something about the young trainer he found very attractive. Even now, she was standing up for herself but not in an over-the-top display of hysterics or viciousness. He respected her quiet confidence in the face of hardship.

Yet his father had always told him that the evidence never lied, only people did. Was Gina lying?

And Dad had said to never make a judgment on innocence or guilt until all the evidence came in.

"If your brother is truly after you as you've stated, then you should be where you can be protected."

Earl narrowed his gaze on Shane. "She's been questioned. She's innocent until proven guilty. But you're right, she's in danger and needs protection. That'll be your job, Weston."

Oh, man. He hadn't expected to be given a protection assignment. What did he know about being a bodyguard? He'd trained to be out on the streets, catching criminals and thwarting the schemes of bad people. Surely the chief would want someone with more experience to protect Gina. "Are you sure—"

Earl arched one eyebrow as he cut Shane off. "Yes." There was no room for argument in his tone. Then Earl turned his gaze to Gina. "Don't leave town."

Gina lifted her chin. "No, sir, I won't."

Sophie and Ryder joined them. They'd managed to corral the puppies and now each had one in their arms.

"Where's Marco, the third pup?" Gina asked.

"He's probably inside," Sophie said. "I'll round him up and put him in the crate with these two."

"I didn't see a third puppy when I was inside," Ryder said. "Just these ones."

For a moment no one said anything. Then Shane asked, "Could the killer have taken the puppy?"

*Shane thinks I could have killed Veronica!* Standing beneath the bright glare of the flood lamps that illuminated the crime scene in garish detail, Gina curled her fingers into fists and pressed them into the sides of her thighs. She stared at Shane as he stepped away to call another rookie—his roommate, James Harrison—and wanted to scream. How could he think she'd do something so horrible?

But it wasn't as if he knew her, despite their having spent every day together the past twelve weeks. She knew he took his job very seriously, but really?

She inwardly scoffed. What did it matter anyway? So what if the handsome officer had invaded her daydreams over the past weeks. She couldn't, wouldn't, allow herself to develop deep feelings for him. There was too much risk involved. And risky behavior was something she avoided. Besides, now that his training had ended, he'd be moving on. As he should.

Forcing her mind away from what Shane thought of her, she tried to focus on the missing puppy, Marco. But the fear of Tim and where he might be made it difficult. His presence loomed, a dark shadow at the edges of her awareness.

"Maybe Marco got out of the yard," she said, careful to keep her gaze from where Veronica lay in the dirt. Even though the coroner had covered her body with an opaque plastic sheet, Gina didn't want to look. The image of Veronica's lifeless eyes, so like Gina's father's after Tim had killed him, would haunt her nightmares for a long time to come.

Instead, out of habit—or out of self-defense,

as her therapist would most likely observe—she shifted her gaze to the wooded area behind the training center. "The puppy could be in the woods."

So could Tim. A shiver chased the thought across her flesh.

She turned to look down the residential street flanking one side of the center. "Or in someone's backyard. Maybe he ran out and someone took him in?"

"Good thought," the chief said. "As soon as Harmon arrives I'll have him start searching for the pup. The woods will have to wait until daybreak since we don't have the manpower to spare."

"The puppy has a distinct black circular marking on its head, between its fawn-colored ears," Gina told them. "He's a very sweet puppy. They all are."

"Is there a way to check if Veronica chipped the dogs? That would give us a better time line for when she was…killed." Ryder nearly dropped the wiggling pup. "Hey, settle down."

"That's Ricky," Gina told him. "Mrs. Foxcroft insisted on naming the puppies. Marco was named after one of her relatives who founded Desert Valley. The other two are Ricky and Lucy. She loves the *I Love Lucy* show."

Sophie stroked Lucy's head. "I can check to see if they're chipped. It will only take a moment. But we'll have to go inside."

The chief asked Ryder, "Did you find the scene of the crime?"

"Yes, sir," Ryder replied. "The trail of blood leads to the clinic."

"That's where Veronica would have done the chipping," Gina interjected, sick at the thought of Veronica facing down Tim alone.

"Any sign of a struggle?" Sophie nuzzled Lucy. The pup squirmed in her arms, clearly wanting to be set free again.

Ryder shook his head. "Not in the clinic. My guess is she knew the killer. Otherwise, Veronica would have fought. She's— She was a fighter."

Gina's heart thumped. "She didn't know Tim."

No one in Desert Valley even knew she had a brother.

She'd been careful to keep her past buried. She hadn't wanted the attention. She'd tried to keep a low profile. With her brother on the loose, having escaped police custody and out for vengeance after she'd turned him in for killing their father, she'd hoped and prayed he'd never find her. But he had. How? What had led him to Desert Valley?

"But if he came in asking for you and she didn't think he was a threat…" Shane said, rejoining them and pulling her from her thoughts.

Gina frowned, hating that he was right. Tim could be charming when he wanted to be. He could have surprised Veronica, not given her time to defend herself. Gina's insides twisted. How had Tim found her? How many more lives would Tim ruin before he was stopped? Cold sweat broke out on her neck.

Ryder eyed Gina's fellow trainer and friend Sophie with a speculative gleam in his blue eyes. "Where were you tonight?"

Sophie's gaze hardened. "Home. Alone. As I said, I heard over the police radio that something was going on here."

"Which means the press will have heard, as well," the chief interjected. "No doubt a reporter from the *Canyon County Gazette* is on the way. Let's secure this crime scene pronto." He looked to the coroner. "Randolph, what do you think?"

"My preliminary examination supports that the scene of the crime was elsewhere. Rigor hasn't set in yet, so estimated time of death is within the past hour. There are two visible wounds in the chest, consistent in size and shape to what one would expect to see from a bullet. No exit wounds. Once the…"

He faltered as he straightened. In such a small town as Desert Valley, it was conceivable that Randolph had known Veronica. Since Desert Valley didn't have a crime lab, everything including the victim's body would be transported to Flagstaff and processed there. Gina considered that a blessing for the visibly shaken coroner.

Randolph removed his gloves and tossed them into a plastic bag before plucking his thick glasses from his nose. His dark eyes were sad. "Once the autopsy is performed you'll be provided a conclusive cause of death."

Ryder gestured to the dark trail of blood. "What I can't determine is if Veronica was dragged out here or if she crawled out on her own steam before she died. Even with the lamps it's too dark to see impressions in the dirt. In the morning we'll have a better idea of what happened."

"She might've been trying to find help," Gina said. "Though why wouldn't she use the phone? Either the center's landline or her cell?"

"Good questions," the chief said. "Ryder, I want you to take the lead in this investigation."

Clearly surprised, Ryder nodded. "Yes, sir. I'll do everything possible to find Veronica's murderer."

"What's the story with your brother, anyway?" Shane asked Gina, drawing everyone's attention. "Why was he in police custody?"

Gina bit her lip, loathing to air her sordid family history in public. She'd purposely kept her personal information vague when asked, but with everyone staring at her, waiting for an explanation, she had no choice but to explain.

"He suffers from schizoaffective disorder. Our father enrolled him in an experimental program two years ago, but Tim didn't want to go. He was in one of his manic phases and had a psychotic break. He killed—" Her voice wavered. "He killed our father with Dad's own service weapon. The police arrested him, but he escaped custody and fled. He blames me for calling the police and turning him in. Now he's here and has made it very clear he wants to kill me, too."

"That's rough," Ryder said. The puppy in his arms licked his face.

Earl put his hand on her shoulder. "We won't let anything happen to you."

Shane's gaze was skeptical. He didn't believe her. And that hurt.

Sophie snuggled Lucy closer. "If Tim has Marco, do you think he'd hurt him?"

Gina put a hand over the pain exploding in her heart. "I hope not." She gave a helpless shrug. "He has killed before, so I'm not certain of anything when it comes to Tim."

"James is headed to your house," Shane said. "As soon as he gives the all clear, we'll head over so you can change."

Gina looked at Sophie and admitted softly to her friend, "I'm afraid to go home."

"Weston will accompany you." The chief squeezed her shoulder.

Her stomach somersaulted. For the past twelve weeks she and Shane had danced around each other and the attraction that, at times, was so strong between them she grew light-headed. Like she was now as she stared into his emerald gaze.

But apparently the attraction had been one-sided. Just as well. She had homicidal tendencies floating in her genetic soup. A fact she couldn't deny, nor would she burden anyone else with it.

Besides, Shane was leaving town as soon as he was given his assignment. She'd be a fool to ever let herself become attached to him.

"You'll be safe with Harrison and Weston." The chief's voice was reassuring and confident, yet did nothing to assure her.

Would she be safe with them? Would they be safe with her? Or would they become two more victims of Tim's rage?

She didn't want to go anywhere with Shane if he thought she could be a murderer.

A taunting thought screamed through her. *You share the same DNA as Tim. Why wouldn't he wonder if you're capable of murder, too?*

# THREE

Giving herself a mental shake, Gina tore her gaze away from Shane and focused on Sophie. She liked the other trainer; they got along well. Veronica had intimated that Sophie had somehow failed as a cop, but Gina had been careful not to ask many questions about what had brought Sophie to Desert Valley. Not that Gina wasn't curious, but she'd figured she'd better not probe if she didn't want anyone probing into her past. "Can you take me?"

Sophie winced. "I'm going to need to stay here and see what else might be missing besides our little Marco."

Gina blew out a frustrated breath. "I understand. You should also check the vet's prescription drug supply next door. If Tim needed money, he could sell the dog and any drugs he stole." She glanced at Shane as he answered his ringing phone.

After a moment, he hung up and said, "Officer Harrison says your house is clear."

She was boxed in with no other option. "Okay, fine. Let's go."

She hurried away. Each step that took her closer to her house pounded another shard of fear into her. What if Tim had slipped past them and was waiting for her to return home? What if he was there now hurting James Harrison? She shook her head to dislodge the horrid thought.

"Hey, wait up," Shane called as he hurried toward her, Bella trotting at his side.

She slowed, keeping her gaze alert for any sign of Tim. Having Shane and Bella close did help keep the terror from overwhelming her. She whistled for the puppy. "Marco!"

Shane fell into step beside her. Bella stayed at his heel on his other side. He swept his flashlight over the bushes and at the trees. "Marco, here, boy."

Worry for the pup churned in Gina's stomach. Predators such as coyotes, mountain lions, bobcats and bears roamed the area. Though most stayed clear of the town, there had been enough sightings for Gina to know the small puppy wouldn't stand a chance on his own in the wild.

She knocked on every front door between the training yard and her house, but no one had seen Marco. He must have run in the opposite direction. Or toward the woods at the back of the training center.

Though the moon was high and the clouds had moved on, there was no way to track the puppy at night. She shivered, grateful for Shane's presence. His calmness helped to ground her fears and keep her coherent as she woke her neighbors with her questions about the missing puppy.

As they neared her house, Shane said, "For the record, I don't want to believe you killed Veronica."

"For the record, I didn't kill her," Gina shot back with frustration. "I may have had my issues with her, but I would never hurt another living soul."

At least she prayed not. But the fear was always at the edge of her consciousness. "I can't imagine how Marian Foxcroft will react to learning one of the puppies she donated to the center has gone missing."

"Ellen's mother, right?"

"Yes." Ellen Foxcroft was another graduate from the same training session as Shane. "Marian has a purebred German shepherd." Acid burned in Gina's tummy. "I pray we find Marco. I can only imagine how upset Marian will be."

"It was very generous of Mrs. Foxcroft to give the puppies to the training center," Shane commented.

"Yes. Very generous. However, Veronica was certain Marian's intention wasn't pure benevolence." A wave of sadness washed over her. Veronica had had her faults, but she hadn't deserved to die.

Shane stopped walking and drew her into the shadows of a mesquite tree. "How so?"

His closeness sent her senses spinning. She backed up a step and bumped up against the tree. "I'm not sure. Veronica could be so caustic at times that I rarely paid any attention to her snide remarks. But she'd said something to the effect that Marian holds her donations over the center and expects something in return."

"Like what?" He braced a hand on the tree near her head, surrounding her in a warm cocoon.

Her brain became a muddled mess. "I have no idea."

"What's the story with Mrs. Foxcroft?"

Needing distance from him and the confusing effect he had on her, Gina sighed and pushed away from the tree. She really hated telling tales out of turn. But if doing so helped her to earn Shane's trust, then so be it. She stepped back onto the road. "I don't know all the details. Her husband left about five years ago. As far as I know they never divorced. Marian's family dates back to the founding of the town, though I'm not sure where her wealth came from."

"I find it interesting that Ellen became a police officer," Shane said, falling back into step with her. "How did her mother take it?"

"I don't know. Ellen doesn't talk much about her mom." Gina wrinkled her nose. "Marian Foxcroft is…" She struggled to come up with a polite term for the town's feisty matriarch.

"Intimidating?" Shane supplied.

"Yes, exactly."

A car horn beeped. Shane waved a hand. James Harrison, another of the rookies from the most recent graduating training session, pulled up alongside them in his truck. His bloodhound, Hawk, poked his droopy-faced head out of the open passenger window.

James leaned over. "Hey, I was headed to the station." He turned his focus to Gina. "Your house is in shambles. But there was no sign of the intruder."

"That's good," Shane replied.

Gina detested hearing her house had been violated. Obviously, Tim had doubled back just as she'd thought. He could have easily sneaked past them through the woods. And he'd taken out his rage on her home. The thought knocked the breath from her lungs.

If she hadn't been quick enough to get out of the house, if he'd overtaken her at any point, she could very well be dead at this moment. Like Veronica.

Gina clenched her jaw tight to keep from throwing up.

"Is it true? Veronica's dead?" James asked, openly stunned.

"Yes," Shane replied.

James ran a hand through his hair. "That's shocking. I mean, I just saw her this afternoon at the station."

"You'll need to give your statement to Ryder,"

Shane said. "That'll help with the time line leading up to her death."

"Yeah, sure," James said. "Should I head over there now?"

"Not yet," Shane said. "The chief wants us to stick close to Gina." He turned to her. "Which is your house?"

"The one on the corner." She pointed to the end of the street, at the small yellow-and-white two-story cottage that had been her safe haven for two years. She'd had the house painted yellow because the color had been her mother's favorite.

James nodded and turned his truck around before heading back to Gina's and parking in the driveway. As Gina, Shane and Bella approached, James let Hawk out. Bella and Hawk greeted each other.

Shane filled James in on what had happened both here at Gina's house and at the training center.

James whistled through his teeth as he climbed out of his truck. "Wow, this is a lot to process. Veronica had insisted she needed to come to the condo tonight to show me some pointers she thought would be helpful with Hawk."

"That's strange," Gina said. James had done well with his and his bloodhound's training. "What kind of refresher would you need?"

The tall blond and blue-eyed man shook his head. "I have no idea. I thought it was weird, too, but…" He shrugged.

Dismissing the mystery of what Veronica had

been thinking, Gina stepped through the open front door of her little house. She stopped at the sight of her living room. Everything was smashed and broken.

A deep sense of violation and helplessness spread through her, choking off her air. The destruction was senseless.

"The upstairs is just as bad, if not worse," James informed her, with sympathy tingeing his words. Hawk, James's bloodhound, let out a long wail that echoed through the house. Stark fear grabbed Gina by the throat. Had Tim managed to sneak in after James's walk-through?

But the dog turned toward the front door. Something outside the house had him on alert.

Was Tim out there?

Gina moved closer to Shane. He stepped slightly in front of her. The protective gesture melted some of the animosity she'd been feeling toward him.

A woman and a dog entered. Gina let out a relieved breath at the sight of rookie Ellen Foxcroft and her large golden retriever, Carly. After a quick nod of acknowledgment to James and Shane, Ellen turned to Gina. Her normally bright blue eyes were clouded with anxiety. "Are you hurt?"

"No. I'm fine," Gina was quick to assure her. "I'm glad to see you, but why are you here?"

"Mom received a call that something was going on at the training center and then on the way here I heard dispatch say officers were responding to a break-in at your house. I wanted to make sure you were okay."

Gina's stomach twisted as she related the night's events to the rookie.

Visibly shaken, Ellen touched Gina's arm. "That's terrible. And you think your brother killed Veronica?"

"I don't know for sure, but who else could have done it?" She could feel Shane's intense gaze on her. Was he studying her, assessing if she was telling the truth? "Anything's possible with Tim. He never took responsibility for his actions, always blaming his mental illness even though he refused to take his meds."

"That's hard," Ellen said. "I've heard that many times people who go off their medications act out in ways they wouldn't if they were staying on their regimen."

Gina appreciated the other woman's understanding. "Right. But there comes a point when accountability rests with each of us. Tim was cognizant enough of his actions to know right from wrong. And he blames me for calling the police when he killed our father."

Empathy softened Ellen's features. "I'm so sorry for your loss."

"Thank you. It still hurts."

"No matter what degree of loss we experience, it's painful," Ellen said. "But we have to remember that God will never leave us nor forsake us."

Her words wound through Gina. She really wanted to cling to the hope, but sorrow and pain kept her from grabbing on with both hands. She righted a chair.

Ellen glanced at the chaos. "You can't stay here. I'll call my mom and see if she'll mind if you stay with us."

Though Gina was touched by the offer, the thought of going very far from the safety of the police station made her heart race. "I appreciate the offer, but I need to be close to the center."

"You could bunk in the empty bedroom at the condo," James said. "It's only a few blocks from the police station. You'll be safe there with us."

Gina's gaze flew to Shane to see what he thought of the idea. His mouth pressed into a firm line, but he didn't comment.

Hmm. "Shane, would you be okay with that?" she asked.

"It's a good idea that you stay with us," Shane said. "The chief did assign your protection to me."

Gina stared at him. If he thought it a good idea, then why did he look as if he'd just swallowed a lemon? Shaking her head over the perplexing man, she said, "I'll go pack a bag."

"Ellen, would you mind accompanying Gina up-stairs?" Shane asked.

"Not at all." Ellen and Carly escorted Gina to the second floor.

Seeing the damage to her beautiful bedroom

brought Gina to tears. The curtains she'd sewn had been ripped off the rod and shredded. The porcelain doll that had once been her mother's lay smashed on the floor.

James hadn't been kidding when he'd said the upstairs was as trashed as the living room. In what hours ago had been her sanctuary, Tim had taken a knife and shredded everything, including the clothes hanging in the closet.

Deep sadness welled from within. She didn't understand how Tim could be so out of control and mean. Whatever God's purpose was, it was lost on her, which was why she couldn't bring herself to attend church services. How could she worship a God who allowed such travesties?

It was hard enough socializing at the Desert Valley Community Church's singles' potluck and pretending to feel a closeness to God that was absent.

She wasn't even sure why she went every month. Okay, that wasn't true. She went because some part of her hoped to fall in love. Yet she turned down any offers of dates, too afraid to allow someone into her life. Nuts, right?

What was that saying by Albert Einstein? The definition of insanity was doing the same thing over and over again and expecting different results.

She snorted. Maybe she was more like her brother than she wanted to admit. Carly's wet nose nudged her hand. Absently, she stroked the dog's head.

It wasn't as if the town of Desert Valley, located in the northwest part of Arizona, was big enough for her to meet someone new. After living in the small community for nearly two years, she knew most everyone on a first-name basis.

The revolving door on the K-9 training center didn't lend itself to finding romance. The rookies arrived for their twelve-week session then left, taking assignments that took them all over the state of Arizona. Most of them held little interest for her.

She mentally scoffed. Who was she kidding?

Shane Weston had caught her attention. But he wasn't staying. He'd made that clear from day one.

Maybe she was a glutton for torturing herself or maybe subconsciously she wasn't really as interested in becoming half of a whole as she professed. Was she deluding herself? Wasn't that a sign of mental illness? She'd have to do some research. Maybe check in with her old therapist.

"You okay?"

Ellen's soft question brought Gina's focus back to the closet. She wouldn't find the answer to her life's questions in her destroyed dresses and pantsuits.

"Yes." She stuffed her thoughts away. Taking clothes that Tim had left untouched from the hamper, she quickly changed out of her soiled outfit, then handed it to Ellen, who put the clothes into the evidence bag.

Ellen's gaze raked over the sliced and diced garments barely hanging on the hangers. "Whoa."

Gina waved a dismissive hand. "This can all be replaced."

"If you need to go shopping in Flagstaff, I'm always up for a trip to the city," Ellen said with a sympathetic smile.

Carly left Gina to go stand beside her mistress.

Appreciating Ellen's attempt at levity, Gina returned her smile. "Thanks. I'll keep that in mind."

Gina grabbed her suitcase from beneath the bed, gathered her toiletries and dumped them in the bottom of the suitcase. "Your mother must be very proud of you for having completed your training."

Ellen made a noise halfway between a laugh and a scoff. "Mom's never been behind me being a police officer."

"I'm sorry to hear that. I think you'll make a great one." Gina pulled the rest of the clothes from the laundry basket, figuring she'd wash everything at the condo. Her pulse skipped a beat as she thought of sharing a living space with Shane. She ruthlessly squelched her reaction.

And James, she reminded herself. She wouldn't be alone with Shane. And she'd have her own suite. Thankfully.

"Thanks. But it's the story of my life." Ellen's gaze took on a faraway look. "There's a lot that Mom and I don't see eye to eye on."

Sensing something painful behind the other woman's words, Gina put a hand on Ellen's arm to offer what comfort she could. "But you have her and you two love each other." Gina would give anything to have her mother back. Even for just a moment.

Ellen nodded, but doubts lingered in her blue eyes. "Yes. You're right. But I'm looking forward to being assigned far from Desert Valley. You know that old saying, absence makes the heart grow fonder. I'm hoping that will prove to be true."

Gina hurt for the apparent rift between Ellen and Marian.

"Ladies?" Shane called from the bottom of the stairs. "Do you need some help?"

Gina rolled her eyes. "Impatient much?" she muttered.

Ellen smiled. "It's a guy thing."

"Or just a Shane thing," Gina quipped as she zipped the suitcase. She'd noticed during training that he wanted things to progress at a swifter pace. She'd had to remind him training was a process that couldn't be rushed. She supposed he was anxious to get back to the city. Apparently country life wasn't to his liking.

Gina picked up her suitcase and followed Ellen and Carly down the stairs. She retrieved her cell phone from the charger sitting on the hall table. The one she hadn't had time to grab before running for her life.

Once they were out of the house, Gina thanked Ellen for her help. She climbed into James's truck along with Shane. The two dogs hopped into the canopied truck bed and lay down. James latched the tailgate in place but left the windows open for airflow.

Sandwiched between the two men, Gina could hardly believe her life had taken such a drastic turn in such a short amount of time. Her brother had attacked her, her boss had been murdered, and now she'd been displaced from her home and put under the protection of two handsome men. One who made her heart flutter despite how much she tried to quell her attraction.

Could her life get any more complicated?

A loud *thunk* echoed inside the cab of the truck, sending a jolt of fear through Gina. "What was that?"

# FOUR

James brought the truck to an abrupt halt and jumped out, leaving the driver's-side door open.

Shane's heart hammered in his chest. He gripped Gina's hand. His gaze raked over her. "Are you hurt?" He had to yell over the frantic barking of the two dogs in the truck bed.

Her hazel eyes were wide and her pretty face pale, but otherwise she appeared unharmed. "No. I don't think so."

Ellen's vehicle pulled up behind them, her headlights shining through the window.

James jumped back in the cab of the truck. "An arrow," he said as he hit the gas. The truck shot forward.

The two words sent a shiver down Shane's spine.

James drove quickly to the police station, with Ellen close behind, and parked in front of the doors. Shane jumped out and hustled Gina inside. Bucks was manning the desk.

"Keep an eye on her," Shane told the officer before running back outside just as James dropped the tailgate and both dogs jumped out. Bella ran to Shane's side.

Shane moved closer to see what had struck the truck. Protruding from the front of the truck bed, just below the rear window, was indeed an arrow. But not the kind found in archery. This was steel, a long bolt with yellow fetching. The kind meant for killing.

The blood drained from Shane's head. He gripped the edge of the truck bed. A couple of inches higher and the bolt would have gone through the window, right into Gina's skull.

Or the projectile could have easily hit one of the dogs. But thankfully, both were uninjured.

Was this the work of Gina's brother? Why would he change weapons from a gun to a crossbow? Hadn't Gina said he'd had a knife, too? They had a well-armed fugitive in their town.

James hooked Hawk to his lead. The bloodhound lifted his nose to the air and howled. "We're going hunting. The keys are in the ignition if you need to move the truck. Hawk and I will meet you at the condo."

"Be careful," Shane advised.

"Roger that." James and Hawk took off, trailing a scent, and disappeared from view.

Ellen approached from where she'd parked her vehicle. "Did you see the shooter?" Shane asked.

"Shooter?" Her blues eyes darted to the arrow then back to him. "Is Gina okay?"

"Yes, she's inside." Shane moved back to the cab and ran a hand over the back of the seat. Applying a little pressure on the backrest, he could feel the sharp tip of the arrow where it had gone through the metal of the truck. So close. He breathed out a prayer of thanksgiving.

Another inch and the arrow absolutely would have skewered Gina in the back.

Clearly someone wanted her dead. It seemed her story about her brother was true.

Gina came out of the police station with Bucks hot on her heels. "Someone tell me what's happening."

Shane glared at Bucks.

He raised his hands. "Hey, I couldn't stop her."

Gina spotted the arrow sticking out of the back of the cab and gasped. The moon's glow shone on her face, creating shadows in the contours of her cheekbones. "Do you think… Did Tim do this?"

He wouldn't sugarcoat the truth. "Unless there's someone with a vendetta against the trainers, which I doubt, I can't think of anyone else who wants you dead. Can you?"

She wrapped her arms around her middle. "No. And I didn't kill Veronica. Tim must have. Don't you see that?"

"Come on, let's get you back inside." Shane placed his hand to the small of her back. He didn't like her standing outside, making herself an easy target if her brother had followed them to the station. "I'm sorry I jumped to a hasty conclusion."

Gina's glance lanced across his face like a laser. "So you believe me now?"

*Innocent until proven guilty.* The evidence to suggest she was the culprit was circumstantial at best. It was more likely that her brother had killed Veronica. "Yes."

Some of her tension visibly released.

Once they were all in the lobby of the station, Ellen logged in the evidence bag filled with Gina's clothes and then said good-night before heading home. Keeping Gina close, Shane asked Bucks to dust the arrow for prints.

"Hey, I don't work for you," the older officer grumbled.

The chief stepped out of his office. "What's the trouble?"

Bucks shot Shane a venomous look. "He'll explain." He marched off.

"On our way here from Gina's house a bolt from a crossbow pierced the cab," Shane explained. "I asked Officer Bucks if he'd dust the arrow for prints."

Chief Jones's jaw hardened. "Seems your brother is determined."

"Yes, sir," Gina murmured as she sank onto a bench.

Bella went to her and put her chin on Gina's knees.

"Thank the Lord above none of you were hurt," Earl said. He'd seemed to age in the past few hours. The lines around his mouth and eyes were deeper, adding to his haggard look. Undoubtedly, Veronica's murder was hitting the man hard. "This has been a horrific night for our town. We've seen more crime in the past six hours than we've had in five years…since Melanie Hayes's unsolved murder."

Ryder Hayes's wife, Melanie, had been gunned down on a wooded path near the couple's house on the eve of the big annual Canyon County Police Dance and Fundraiser. Robbery was the suspected motive, since Melanie's purse had gone missing.

Shane had also heard about two other mysterious deaths. Each on the night of the annual dance and fundraiser event, and each a year apart. But both fatalities had been deemed accidents.

The chief rubbed his chin. "Tonight makes retirement that much more enticing."

Back home in Flagstaff, this night would have seemed tame to Shane's dad and brothers. "Did the canvass around the training center yield anything useful in determining who killed Veronica?"

Earl held up a hand. "So far no one heard any shots fired or saw anyone come or go from the center."

"Has anyone turned in the missing puppy?" Gina asked.

"Unfortunately, no," the chief replied.

Gina's arms wrapped around her middle as if

holding herself together. The tender skin beneath her eyes appeared bruised from fatigue and her face was pale.

Empathy twisted in Shane's gut, despite his need to stay emotionally detached. First being attacked in her house by her crazed brother, then stumbling upon Veronica's dead body. It was obvious she loved the animals she worked with and they loved her, if Bella's actions were any indication. No doubt the thought of the little German shepherd puppy running loose outside where wildlife could prey on it weighed heavily on Gina's slim shoulders.

"Was Sophie able to determine if the other two puppies were chipped?" Gina asked.

"They were," Earl replied. "Chipped and registered to Veronica with the training center's address just as we'd expect."

"Hopefully, someone will pick up the pup and take him to the vet," Gina said. "If Veronica was able to get him chipped then the vet will find the chip and contact the center."

"I'll give the vet a heads-up," the chief said.

Bucks returned a few moments later. "I got a partial. I'll run it through IAFIS."

Shane hoped the FBI's national fingerprint database would provide a visual of Tim Perry. Or whoever had handled the arrow. Shane struggled to believe no one had known Gina had a brother to begin with, let alone one who was a criminal. Was the shooter the same person who'd killed Veronica?

Or was there more than one villain running around Desert Valley? That seemed too much of a stretch.

"Let's finish our discussion in my office," Earl said, ushering Shane, Bella and Gina inside.

The chief had just settled into his chair behind his desk when there was a knock on the doorjamb. James and Hawk entered the office, looking grim.

Shane gave him a questioning look.

James shook his head. "Hawk tracked a scent but lost it on a street two blocks away from Gina's house. The shooter must have jumped into a car and taken off."

"Did you get a look at the archer?" Earl asked.

"No, never caught a glimpse of him," James said.

Earl looked at Shane. "But you're sure it was her brother?"

"Hard to say without confirmation," Shane said. "But without any other suspects..."

The chief considered him a moment. "Okay." He focused on Gina. "Where will you be staying? Obviously you can't return to your home until we have your brother in custody."

"Sir, Gina is going to move into the empty room at the rookies' condo," Shane stated. He met Gina's gaze. She arched one delicate eyebrow. Okay, maybe he shouldn't have answered for her.

Earl nodded approval. "Good." He settled his gaze on Gina once again. "We'll find your brother. Or whoever did this. No one can hide in Desert Valley for long."

"Thank you, sir." Her voice was tight. She turned her gaze on Shane. "I'd like to keep the puppies with me if possible."

The anxiety in her hazel eyes tugged at him. If having the two pups close comforted her, then... "Of course. We'll swing by the training center and pick them up."

She gave him a grateful smile as she stifled a yawn.

"You all go and get some rest," the chief said. "You won't do anyone any good if you're too exhausted to be of use."

Shane escorted Gina from the station. They took James's truck to the training center. Sophie had crated the puppies and had locked up the center for the night. Gina used her key card to enter the building.

They gathered the puppies and their crates, along with their beds, water and food bowls, and put them in the back of James's truck. Gina held both pups on her lap during the ride to the condo.

James parked in the carport stall reserved for the rookies' unit. He grabbed her bag from the back and led the way to the front door. Shane carried the pups' accoutrements and brought up the rear with Gina and the puppies between them.

Once inside, Shane showed Gina to the room at the end of the short hall. He arranged the crates side by side along the far wall beneath the window facing the queen-size bed covered with a deep burgundy comforter.

Gina set the puppies down on their respective beds and left the crate doors open. They immediately went to sleep, obviously tuckered out from their run in the yard and the move to the condo.

"Shouldn't you shut the crate doors?" Shane asked.

"I will when I'm ready to go to sleep, but for now I want them to feel safe inside their crates and safe to leave, as well. The crate needs to become their safe haven. Locking them in too soon can be traumatic."

Her concern for the puppies was touching. Given she'd just lived through a very dramatic and dangerous situation, she was holding it together really well. Assuming she was telling him the truth, which seemed more likely with every passing moment. His admiration and respect for her increased. How had he questioned whether she could be guilty of hurting Veronica?

"The place comes furnished," Shane explained, to battle the discomforted way she made him feel. "Each room is a suite. Housekeeping launders all the linens between the training sessions. The bedding's clean and there are towels in the bathroom cabinet."

"Thank you," Gina said. "I appreciate all you're doing for me and the puppies."

Her teeth tugged on her bottom lip. She looked

so vulnerable. Blood surged through his veins and his gut tightened. It was all he could do not to step closer and gather her in his arms. He'd been attracted to her from the beginning, but this was more intense and focused. The disturbing urge had him backing away. The last thing he wanted was to become emotionally attached to this woman. It was one thing to guard her and help her feel safe, and another entirely to want to make her feel cared for.

"I'll say good-night." He stepped out of the room and shut the door, blocking her from his view. Now if he could only block her from his thoughts as easily.

Gina stared at the door. Confusion swirled through her mind. For a moment, she'd seen something in Shane's expression that had her heart fluttering and her pulse skittering. Interest. There'd been definite interest in his green eyes. Answering attraction flared within her. But then his gaze had shuttered and he'd retreated, leaving her wondering if she'd only imagined the look.

What did it matter? There was no sense in letting herself feel anything for him. For anyone. With her brother back in her life, she was intensely aware that she, too, had the propensity for evil. She shared Tim's DNA. DNA that could be passed on.

She'd never have the family she longed for. What man in his right mind would want to saddle himself with her?

With sadness filling her heart, she filled the dogs' bowls with water and placed them on the bathroom floor, and she sank down on the edge of the bed. She dropped her head into her hands.

What a nightmare her life had become. Tim was attempting to follow through on his threat to kill her. She didn't understand what purpose Tim had for wanting her dead. It wouldn't change the fact that he was wanted for murdering their father.

That he hadn't succeeded in killing her so far was a blessing.

It hurt her heart to believe Veronica had died because of her. She had no doubt Tim had killed her boss. What other explanation could there be?

"Oh, Lord, please. I…" She didn't know what to say or how to pray.

She wanted to ask God to stop her brother, yet the words wouldn't come. They felt like rocks stuck in her throat. Would God even hear her? She was so used to being disappointed she was afraid to try anymore.

She lay back, wishing the oblivion of sleep would take her away, but her mind was buzzing with all that had transpired. The image of Veronica's lifeless eyes staring at the sky tormented her. Worry for the missing puppy scraped her nerves raw.

"Please let us find Marco, Lord," she whispered, finally finding some reserve of faith. She curled on her side. The sleeping puppies looked so peaceful.

So vulnerable. They needed her now. She had to be strong for their sake.

Her mouth felt like cotton. She needed water. She rose to check the bathroom for a cup and found none. She left the bedroom to pad barefoot to the kitchen in search of a glass. As she passed the living room, she noticed Shane sitting on the couch, brushing Bella, who sat at his feet, obviously enjoying the attention to her coat.

Light from the gas fireplace played in the dark strands of Shane's hair, making them appear more blue than black. Once again the pull of longing lurched at her and attraction flickered through her. He was so handsome and capable. And she appreciated the fact that he'd apologized for jumping to an assumption of her guilt before knowing all the facts. She figured it was probably hard for him to admit he was wrong. But he'd owned up to his mistake and that meant a lot to her.

Plus, she had enjoyed working with him during their training. Even if he was a bit impatient with the progress, he'd never once taken that impatience out on Bella or Gina. But Gina had seen the frustration in his eyes and the tension in his shoulders. She wasn't sure what had driven him. Wasn't sure she wanted to know. Getting too close to her protector wouldn't be smart.

She paused, contemplating turning back. But then Shane's gaze lifted and met hers.

He swiftly rose, the brush dropping to the floor. "Are you okay?"

The concern in his tone caused warmth to flow through her. Bella cocked her head and stared at Gina as if waiting for her answer, as well.

She smiled. "I'm fine. I just wanted a glass for water."

He nodded and resumed his seat. "Glasses are in the cupboard to the right of the sink."

Bella lay down at his feet, apparently reassured that all was well.

She filled a glass from the tap. She drank the cool liquid and then refilled the glass to take to her room. She halted on the threshold of the living room. "Why are you still up?"

"Someone has to stand guard. Just in case."

A shiver of dread skated over her flesh. She felt bad that he was losing sleep to keep watch over her. However, she did appreciate his sacrifice. "Have you heard if anyone has reported finding the puppy?"

He shook his head. "No. I'm sure the chief will let us know if he turns up."

Heaviness burdened her heart. Her hand tightened around the glass. "What if no one finds him? What if he's hurt? Or worse?"

"Don't go there. You can't give up hope. We'll find him."

He sounded so confident. She wanted to believe him.

"Tell me about your brother," Shane asked, surprising her. "You're twins. Who's older?"

She moved to sit on the edge of the recliner facing Shane. Warmth from the fire curled around her. "I am, by two minutes and forty-five seconds."

"How long has Tim been…?" His voice faded with uncertainty.

She bit out, "It's okay, you can say it. Mentally ill."

"Right." He sounded uncomfortable. Which was how most people reacted when they learned of Tim's condition. "Mentally ill."

Memories crashed over her, making her heart ache. "The professionals had a hard time diagnosing him. His symptoms were all over the place. No impulse control, inattentive, hyper. But then, as we got older, his mood swings became more erratic, violent even. Our mom was the only one who could handle him." Her heart burned with grief. "She died when we were fifteen."

"I'm sorry. How?"

She appreciated the sympathy in Shane's voice, but she dared not look at him or the tears would break through. Instead she focused on the blue-gold flames in the fireplace. "A car accident. She hit a patch of black ice and slammed into a concrete barrier."

Shane made a sympathetic noise in his throat. Bella shimmied closer and put a paw on her foot as if sensing her sorrow.

Gina leaned down to run her hand over Bella's soft coat. "Tim took Mom's death really hard." Her heart squeezed tight and she straightened. "It was hard on all of us. I miss her every day. Dad did the best he could. But being a cop and a father of two teenagers was a lot for him to handle."

"That's right, you'd said your dad was a police officer. So is mine. And my grandfather was and both brothers are."

"Ah." That explained his drive. He had a family legacy to live up to and he was anxious to get going on his career.

"My dad would be lost without my mom," he said softly.

"Yeah, Dad had a rough time of it. Especially as Tim's behavior became more unpredictable. He hung around some bad influences and started down a very destructive, criminal path. Dad forced him to see a counselor, who passed Tim on to a psychiatrist. But Tim wasn't interested in getting help. I can't blame all of his behavior on his mental illness. He made his choices of his own free will."

"And you? How are you?"

She could feel Shane's gaze on her. More than curiosity drove his question. She understood. This wasn't the first time and it wouldn't be the last someone asked if she, too, had a mental illness. As soon as anyone learned of Tim's disorder, she became suspect, since they were twins. "I saw the same psychiatrist, just in case."

"And?"

"He said I didn't display any of the markers. But no one can guarantee I won't develop a mental disorder one day. It runs in my mother's family." A constant fear that hung over her life like a dark cloud threatening to wash her away and kept her from risking her heart. She wouldn't subject anyone to that uncertainty.

"Did the psychiatrist have any idea why your brother would be affected and you seemingly aren't?"

She shrugged. "Even non-twin siblings have a ten-percent chance of developing the same disorders."

"That's a pretty low percentage. Chances are you'll never suffer the same fate."

She wished she could count on his words to be true. "But there is still a chance. No one can make any guarantees one way or the other."

"One of God's many mysteries."

She met his gaze, expecting to see wariness, pity even. Instead, his expression was open and sincere.

"I often wonder why God chose to afflict Tim," she told him. "Dad would say God never made mistakes and that, for reasons we may never know, God made Tim the way he is for a purpose." She couldn't keep the bitterness out of her tone. "I love my brother but I fear him, and have for as long as I can remember. Maybe I inherently knew something wasn't right with him. As for a purpose? That I can't wrap my mind around."

"I agree with your dad. God has a purpose for Tim. For you. I don't know what that purpose is, but He does have one. You have to trust Him."

She cocked her head and studied Shane. She hadn't realized he was a believer. But then again, it wasn't something they'd had reason to discuss during class, and she'd been very careful to keep things work-focused despite how much she wanted to spend time with him outside class. "My dad would have liked you."

The green of his eyes was highlighted by the firelight. "I wish I'd had the chance to meet him."

So did she. A wave of sadness washed over her. She missed her dad so much.

Bella jumped to her feet, her ears back. She let out a loud bark.

A shaft of anxiety tore through Gina. "What's wrong with her?"

Shane rose. "I don't know."

They heard scratching and a long howl. Hawk. James opened his bedroom door. The bloodhound raced through the living room and halted at the sliding glass patio door. Bella joined Hawk, her deep growl ricocheting off the condo's high ceiling. James came into the living room wearing sweats and a T-shirt, his expression sharp with concern and his service weapon in his hand.

From her bedroom, the puppies' excited barks

rang out. Even the pups sensed danger. A shiver of dread ran across her flesh.

Shane touched her shoulder, startling her. "Go to your bedroom and lock the door." He and James moved toward the sliding door.

Gina nearly dropped the glass in her hand. Someone was on the patio. Deep in her heart she knew the trespasser was her brother. Hating the thought of anything happening to Shane or James, she said, "Be careful. You know how dangerous he is."

Shane met her gaze. "I know. Now go."

She hesitated for a second then hurried to her bedroom, locked the door and gathered the pups in her arms. "Oh, Lord, please," she whispered.

There was only one thing for her to do.

Leave Desert Valley and hope this time Tim wouldn't find her.

# FIVE

Shane tempered the adrenaline swamping his system with the knowledge that Gina was safely tucked away behind the locked door of the third bedroom of the condo. They'd made the right call in bringing her here.

He only regretted that he hadn't been the one to suggest it, but the idea of having her underfoot had left him feeling a bit off-kilter.

With the threat of her brother lurking so close, Shane knew his own discomfort had to be relegated to unimportant.

It didn't matter that he found Gina attractive and interesting and that he admired how well she was holding up considering she'd been chased from her home, had discovered her boss's dead body and was being stalked by her evil twin. Not a good day.

Shane reached the kitchen drawer where he'd stashed his service weapon. He grabbed it along with a heavy-duty flashlight, then followed James out the condo's back sliding door.

The dogs ran for the tall fence separating the oblong-shaped patch of grass behind the building and the empty lot beyond. Both dogs sniffed the ground near a spot in the fence where a loose board had been pushed aside.

The acrid odor of tobacco hung in the chilling air. The temperature had dropped as it often did at night in the northwest part of Arizona.

Shane swung the flashlight's beam in sweeping arcs. The light revealed a freshly lit cigarette abandoned on the cement patio floor; a wisp of smoke curled from the smoldering tip in the cool breeze.

How long had the intruder been standing outside? Had it been Gina's brother? Of course. Who else could it have been?

James inspected the fence. "Our guy pried the nails loose."

Which spoke of Tim's determination. Tension knotted Shane's neck muscles. "We need to reattach the board ASAP. And bag and tag this cigarette butt."

James joined him on the patio. "Agreed."

"He's not getting her," Shane vowed. He could feel James's gaze on him but was powerless to keep the fire out of his voice. "I won't let him."

"She's one of the good ones," James observed quietly. "A keeper."

Shane closed his eyes for a moment. "It's not like that."

"Whatever you say." The mocking amusement

in James's voice grated on Shane. "I'll get a baggie for the evidence."

James whistled for Hawk and the two went inside, leaving Shane and Bella standing on the patio.

Bella nudged his thigh.

He scrubbed her behind the ears. "It's okay, girl. We'll get him next time."

Because, unfortunately, Shane knew there would be a next time. He knew in his gut that Tim wouldn't give up. "We'll keep Gina safe."

It was his job to protect her. But he had a feeling he'd have a hard time walking the tightrope between doing his duty and letting himself care too deeply.

He wasn't staying in Desert Valley, and becoming attached to his beautiful charge would only complicate his life in ways he couldn't—wouldn't—allow.

His focus had to be on his career. Distractions like love and romance were for way down the line. He wasn't ready to open himself up for a relationship. Even if the sweet and special dog trainer made his heart pound with longing to amend his plan.

Gina paced the floor of her suite in agitated silence. Three steps right, pivot, three steps left, pivot, repeat. She'd calmed the two puppies, now both chewing on bones she'd grabbed from the training center earlier.

Every noise beyond the confines of her room sent

a jolt of alarm through her, making her heart pound and her blood rush. She was terrified to think Tim had somehow found out where she was so quickly.

Had he been watching, and trailed them to the condo? Would Shane and James capture him? Or would Tim hurt these two brave men who'd promised to protect her? Had Tim put an arrow through Shane? Was Shane even now bleeding and dying because of her?

She squeezed her eyes tight against the onslaught of horrible scenarios that played through her mind. Awfulizing was destructive, as her therapist had advised on numerous occasions. She wasn't even sure that was a real thing but she understood the sentiment behind his caution.

Letting herself spin awful outcomes that hadn't happened as if they had happened only led her to a place of fear. She'd been doing so well here in Desert Valley. All that peace she'd been experiencing had been an illusion, shattered by her brother's reemergence into her life.

"Please, Lord, this time, please don't let anything bad happen to Shane and James."

A soft tap on her door brought her to an abrupt halt. The puppies rushed toward the sound. She stared at the portal, half-afraid to answer the knock.

"Gina?"

Shane's voice echoed inside her head and relief swept through her, making her knees weak. He was alive. That was something to celebrate. But was he hurt?

On shaky limbs she hurried to unlock the door. She scooped up one pup, scooted the other away with her foot and swung the door open. Shane stood there, tall and proud, with worry in his green eyes.

A profound gladness to see him in one piece with no sign of harm washed over her and she nearly launched herself into his arms. To keep from making a fool of herself, she nuzzled the puppy closer to her chest as if doing so would temper her exploding heart. "Did you... Was it Tim?"

Shane shrugged his broad shoulders. "Not sure. But whoever it was—they're gone now."

Letting her chin rest on Lucy's tiny head, she took a deep, calming breath. "Good." She shook her head. "But he won't stop until I'm dead."

Shane stepped into the room and gently took the puppy and set it on the floor. Then his big hands settled on her shoulders. "I'm not going to let anything happen to you."

Warmth from his palms seeped through her lightweight sweater and heated her skin. She gave him a tremulous smile. His concern was so sweet and his determination admirable. But she couldn't put him or anyone else in harm's way, Tim's way, again.

Veronica had paid the ultimate price with her life at Tim's hand. Gina couldn't bear it if another person died because her brother couldn't get to her, especially someone she cared for. "I know you would, but the best thing for me, for everyone, is for me to leave. To disappear again. To start over somewhere else, hopefully somewhere Tim can never find me."

Shane's brows drew together. "You can't run. If you do, you'll be running your whole life. That's no way to live."

"What choice do I have?" she implored, needing to make him understand. "I don't want anyone else to die because of me."

"No one else will," Shane argued. "Now that we know there's a threat out there, we'll all take precautions. Tomorrow we'll put out your brother's photo. Someone in town will have seen him. Desert Valley is a tight-knit community. Any stranger will draw attention."

She moved out of his grasp to where she'd set her suitcase. She held it in front of her like a shield. "I have to leave Desert Valley. There's no other way to keep everyone safe." She glanced at the puppies rolling around on the floor in a cute wrestling match. Her heart hitched. "Will you make sure the puppies are cared for?"

For a long moment, he stayed silent. A muscle in his jaw jumped as he paused, clearly digesting her words. She had no doubt he'd come to the same conclusion that her leaving was the best idea.

Then he shook his head, dispelling her of that notion. "No, leaving is not an option. If you don't trust me to protect you, I'll talk to the chief and have him assign someone else."

"No!" The objection shot from her before she could formulate any coherent thought. "It's not that I don't trust you. I don't want you to get hurt. It's too dangerous."

He smile was tender. He took the suitcase from her and set it on the floor. "I appreciate your concern, but I signed up for danger the minute I applied to the police academy. I'm more troubled by the thought of you fleeing and giving your brother the power to chase you away from the life you've made for yourself here in Desert Valley."

His words rattled through her, stirring up the resentment and anger she'd spent so many years stifling. "I don't want to give Tim any more power over my life. He's taken too much away from me as it is."

"I can't imagine the losses you've suffered."

Empathy dripped from Shane's words, prompting her to say, "For as long as I can remember, he garnered most of the attention from our parents with his bad behavior. There were times when I felt invisible."

"Because they were busy dealing with Tim." His words weren't a question but a statement that pegged the situation exactly.

"The majority of their energy went into helping Tim, keeping him from the destructive behavior he was prone to."

"Which left little time for you."

"Right." He seemed to understand so well. Why was that? "I learned to be self-sufficient. Mom would always say I was more responsible and wiser than most kids my age."

"I'm sure she appreciated that she could rely on you."

Guilt clawed through Gina. Tears pricked her eyes. "And I failed her. The night of her death she'd asked me to keep an eye on Tim while she attended a church function. She'd thought he'd taken his meds that kept him calm, but he hadn't."

Shane enclosed her hand within his. "What happened?"

She curled her fingers around his. "Tim had an episode. He went totally ballistic. I was so afraid of him. Dad was on duty and couldn't be reached. So I hid in the closet and called Mom, begging her to come home. She never did."

Shane squeezed her hand. "I'm so sorry."

"If I hadn't called her…if I'd been able to handle Tim on my own, then Mom wouldn't have been driving so fast and wouldn't have lost control on the black ice, slamming into the concrete divider."

"Her accident wasn't your fault."

She retracted her hand from his grip. Guilt and sorrow settled around her like a veil, dulling her view of the world. "Yes, it was. And now Veronica's dead, too, because of me. I have to leave before Tim kills someone else."

"Gina, listen to me." Shane gripped her shoulders. "Stop being a martyr. You are not responsible for your brother's actions."

Defensiveness reared through her. "That's what you think I'm doing? Being a martyr?"

His expression softened and his voice gentled. "Yes. You're smarter and stronger than you let yourself believe."

The compliment bounced off her as indignation took hold. How dare he say she was being a martyr? He didn't know her well enough to make that kind of assessment.

Yet something inside of her stilled. Was she being a martyr? Maybe that was how her mental illness would surface. She shuddered.

"Leaving isn't the answer," he insisted with grim determination tingeing his tone. "You have the whole Desert Valley Police Department behind you. Let us do our jobs. We'll protect you. And arrest Tim and put him away where he can't hurt anyone ever again."

"But you're leaving come Monday morning. You won't be here to protect me."

A frown pinched his eyebrows together. "Ryder will be here and the chief. They are good and dedicated police officers. They will protect you. But hopefully, we'll catch Tim by Monday morning."

Against her will fat tears welled in her eyes. She desperately wanted to believe in Shane. Believe he could triumph over Tim. "But what if he hurts you or someone else?" She laid her hands on his broad chest. His heart beat strong beneath her palms. "I couldn't take it."

"We have to trust God."

Staring into Shane's green eyes, she dug deep for faith and trust and hope. From the far reaches of her soul she found the courage to nod. She blinked to clear her tears.

She'd stay and stand her ground. She'd let the men and women of the Desert Valley Police Department protect her. She'd trust Shane.

And she'd pray every single moment for their safety.

Because if another person died because of her, she would shrivel up and die herself.

By Monday morning, Tim hadn't surfaced. He was still on the loose and Gina's nerves were stretched taut. Shane and Bella escorted Gina and the puppies to the training center to begin the puppies' training. As they entered, Gina noticed the caution signs indicating the linoleum floors had recently been mopped and were slick. She scooped up Lucy, holding her in a cuddling position against her chest. She said to Shane, "Can you carry Ricky? Their nails will slip on the wet floor."

"Of course." He picked up Ricky and held him like a football. She suppressed a smile. Dressed in jeans that hugged his muscular legs and a short-sleeved, colorful checked button-down shirt, he and the puppy made a handsome pair. One would never know he was an officer of the law, except for the service weapon holstered at his hip on the belt encircling his trim waist and the gold shield butted up next to the holster.

Though she'd dressed in her normal work attire of lightweight stain-resistant pants and a pink T-shirt, she sort of wished she were dressed a little more attractively. She nearly groaned at her silliness. She wasn't trying to attract the handsome rookie.

They moved farther into the center, past the bathing stations and the room they used to chip the canines. The place where Veronica had faced her attacker.

Thankfully all traces of the devastating violence that had occurred here were gone. Mopped up and wiped away. No doubt the chief had a crew of crime and trauma scene decontamination come in from Flagstaff and take care of the aftermath of Veronica's death once the Flagstaff crime scene unit had finished collecting evidence.

Gina's stomach lurched as the horrible scenario of Veronica being shot by Tim played inside her head, like a movie clip. Her mouth went dry. Tears burned the backs of her eyes. Lucy licked her face, breaking the hold her imagination had on her mind.

"You okay?"

Shane's gently asked question forced her feet to move. "I will be when Tim is caught."

In the common space, Gina was grateful to see the other trainer, Sophie, was already at the center.

"Hey, I didn't expect to see you here today." Sophie leaned on the mop in her hand and dressed in blue coveralls. Her blond hair was twisted up in back.

Heart beating in her throat, Gina managed to say, "You didn't clean up…?"

Sophie's eyes widened. "Oh, no. That's not in my job description." She visibly shuddered. "I was keeping busy by cleaning the indoor yard and mopping out the bath station."

A job they rotated doing. Gina blew out a relieved breath. She'd hate to think her fellow trainer had had to be responsible for the cleanup of the crime scene.

"Did you get any rest?"

Sophie's question didn't surprise Gina. She'd seen the dark circles under her eyes in the mirror. There wasn't much she could do to hide them. "I managed to get a little sleep. You don't mind that we're here, do you?"

"Not at all." Sophie scratched Lucy behind the ear. "You can let them in the training yard. It's clean and ready for use. I'm just surprised you're ready to be here."

They moved into the indoor training yard. The large space was filled with agility equipment placed strategically throughout. Against one wall was a set of cabinets that housed treats and toys; lining another was a row of benches with cubbyhole storage for the trainers and the handlers to use for their personal effects. She set the puppies down. Bella ran roughshod over the two rambunctious pups.

"We had a bit of trouble," Shane told Sophie, who'd followed them into the yard. "Someone, presumably her brother, broke through the fence to spy on the condo late last night."

Concern darkened Sophie's gold-tinted eyes. "But you're all okay?"

Gina nodded. "Yes. Shane and James and Bella and Hawk chased him off." She couldn't keep a shudder from rippling down her spine.

"The chief has called a meeting over at the station," Shane said, his reluctance to leave obvious.

"It's customary on the Monday after a training session ends for the chief to hand out the rookies' new assigned police station," Gina told him. The thought of Shane leaving bit into her, making her admit to herself she didn't want him to go. Because he was protecting her. Not because she liked him.

Okay, she did like him, but her feelings didn't go any deeper than that.

Shane's green eyes grew troubled. "Right, but I don't feel comfortable leaving you here."

"Sophie's armed," Gina pointed out. "I'll be fine. You go. Find out if anyone has found Marco."

"Don't worry, Shane," Sophie added. "I'll make sure the door is locked behind you."

"You have your cell phone?" Shane asked Gina.

She tugged the device from the training pouch at her waist. "Right here. And you're on speed dial. So is the station."

"Maybe I should leave Bella with you," Shane said.

As sweet as that offer was, she couldn't let him. "She's your partner, you can't leave her behind," Gina said. "I'll be busy training Ricky and Lucy. We'll be fine."

She let out a soft whistle to draw the two puppies' attention. They raced over. Ricky chewed on the laces of Shane's black boots while Lucy sniffed the floor, following a scent toward the treat cabinet. Lucy obviously already had the instinct to track. Good.

Gina looked forward to working with her. It would take more effort, however, to figure out the correct specialty for Ricky. He seemed more inclined to chew and play than work. But she had high hopes for him.

Just as she did for Marco. Her heart ached with worry.

However, it'd be one to two years before any of the dogs were ready to begin the rigorous K-9 training demanded of the canine officer and his handler. First the pups needed to learn basic commands as well as potty training. As demonstrated when Ricky lifted his leg.

"Hey!" Shane exclaimed and jumped out of the way.

"I'll mop up the mess," Sophie said through suppressed laughter.

Shane shook his head and moved away from the puddle. "I'm glad Bella came with manners already in place."

Gina scooped Ricky up. "He'll learn. He's still very young, you know. I hope someone finds Marco soon."

"I talked to the chief this morning," Shane told her. "He gave the vet a heads-up in case anyone brings Marco to her and sent Officer Donaldson out to search again."

She was sure the veterinarian, Tanya Fowler, would be quick to act if anyone brought the lost little puppy to the veterinary clinic. "I'd like to help search for Marco."

Shane shook his head. "We can't risk you being out in the open. You're safer here."

Though he was right, it chafed that she had to be basically a prisoner in the training center until her brother was caught. She sighed. "You better get to your meeting."

He nodded. "Lock the door behind me."

She followed him to the training center exit.

He paused halfway out the door. Bella stopped next to him as she'd been taught to do. "I won't be long."

"We'll be fine." She waved him and Bella out. When she slid the lock in place, the noise echoed inside her head. For a second she had the strangest urge to run after Shane. His presence made her feel safe and cared for. Without him close, she felt exposed, vulnerable.

She was being ridiculous. She couldn't allow herself to become too reliant on him. He would be leaving for a new town, a life that didn't include her.

Squaring her shoulders, she reminded herself there was no way Tim could get inside the training center. She was safe. And had a job to do.

Holding Ricky up at eye level, she stared into his dark eyes. "Okay, you, time to get busy. I have lots to teach you and your sister."

Shane entered the Desert Valley police station to find the department's secretary balancing a tray with a coffee carafe and a stack of hot cups in one hand and a laptop in the other.

"Here, let me," he said, taking the tray. This wasn't the first time he'd offered to help the woman who seemed to have a propensity to juggle many things at one time.

The quiet, plain woman smiled at him. "Thank you, Shane."

He nodded and racked his brain for her name. "Is this for the rookies' meeting?"

"Yes." She gestured down the hall. "This way."

He followed her to a conference room. Bella's nails clicked on the tile floor beside him.

The secretary moved to a corner where there

was a shelf. She opened her laptop and appeared ready to take notes.

After setting the tray on the conference table, Shane took the empty seat next to fellow rookie Tristan McKeller. His dog, a yellow Labrador named Jesse, who specialized in arson and accelerant detection, lay behind his chair. Bella mirrored the other five dogs already in the room by lying down behind Shane's chair.

"Hey," Shane said to Tristan.

"Morning," the former soldier greeted him and then reached for a cup and the carafe. Tristan's tall, muscular frame dwarfed the chair. He wore his brown hair military short. There was no mistaking the worry in his blue eyes. Shane didn't know the full extent of Tristan's story but did know he was raising his teen sister, which was why he'd rented a small house for the duration of their training.

The chief walked in. On his heels was a diminutive woman in a tailored charcoal-colored pantsuit. She wore horn-rimmed glasses over intense dark brown eyes and her auburn hair was cut short at her strong jaw.

Marian Foxcroft.

Shane recognized her from the times she'd come to observe their training at the center. Shane glanced at Ellen Foxcroft at the far end of the table. She had her brown hair pulled back in a braid. She sat ramrod-straight with her eyes on the chief.

Shane imagined it was hard for the rookie knowing her mother disapproved of her chosen field.

The chief's gaze scanned the men and women present. Not only were all of Shane's fellow rookies present, but so were the officers of the Desert Valley Police Department.

Shane wasn't sure why the DVPD officers had been included in this meeting to hear where the rookies would be assigned. He sent up a quick prayer that his request to be sent to the Flagstaff PD came through. The sooner he escaped from the feelings Gina stirred, the better.

"Ladies and gentlemen," the chief intoned in a grave voice. "As you all are aware, Veronica Earnshaw was murdered two nights ago."

From the expressions of some of those sitting around the conference table and leaning against the back wall, not everyone mourned Veronica's passing. But some did. The sadness in Ellen's eyes matched the look in the chief's.

"I know some of you had issues with Veronica in the past," the chief went on to say.

"You got that right," Officer Ken Bucks mumbled.

Chief Jones narrowed his gaze on Bucks. "Whatever problems any of you had with her must be put aside to find her killer."

Bucks had the good grace to flush a bright red.

"Mrs. Foxcroft has generously endowed the department with the funds to hire all five graduating rookies for the foreseeable future. You'll remain with the Desert Valley Police Department until we bring Veronica's killer to justice."

"What?" Ellen exclaimed. "Mother?"

Marian Foxcroft spared her daughter a quick look but made no comment.

Shane exchanged a stunned glance with James. They'd all expected to be assigned to police departments throughout Arizona. Shane wanted to be sent to Flagstaff to become the city cop his family expected him to be, not that he'd been guaranteed the assignment of his choice. None of them had any say in where they ended up. Even still, Shane had made the request at his dad's insistence. Dad wasn't going to be happy about this turn of events—he was already champing at the bit for Shane to take his place in the family business, so to speak.

But as Shane searched his heart, he found he was a bit conflicted, confused even, by how the news didn't stir anger or outrage or even disappointment. Odd.

He shrugged off his lack of reaction and refused to consider its origin. They knew who killed Veronica and would track down Tim Perry soon enough, and then Shane's plan to join the Flagstaff PD could be realized.

"We already have a strong suspect in Veronica's murder," Shane said. "It shouldn't be too difficult to find and arrest Tim Perry."

The chief nodded and picked up a stack of paper

from the head of the table where he stood. "This is the only photo the Mesa PD had of our suspect. Tim Perry is Gina Perry's twin brother. Though there's hardly a resemblance. He is mentally unstable as well as bent on revenge against his sister for turning him in after he shot and killed their father. A Mesa police officer." The chief's gaze settled on Shane. "I trust Gina is at the training center with Sophie."

Shane straightened. "Yes, sir." He trusted the ex-cop to keep Gina safe.

Marian stepped forward. "This latest murder has been very upsetting. I can appreciate that you have a suspect, but other murders have gone unsolved. Veronica bragged to me that this latest batch of recruits were the best and brightest of all her training years."

Her gaze swept over the stunned rookies, lingering slightly on her daughter before she continued. "The county sheriff, the mayor and the governor have given me their assurances that all of you will be given every resource possible not only to bring Veronica's murderer to justice but to solve the cold case murder of Melanie Hayes."

All eyes turned to Ryder. He lifted his chin. "Solving my wife's murder would mean a great deal to my daughter, Lily, and me."

Marian nodded. "No doubt it would. But Melanie's untimely demise isn't the only unsolved crime in Desert Valley."

Shane frowned. He hadn't heard of anything more serious than some robberies.

"What are you referring to, Mother?" Ellen asked.

"The deaths of two rookies in the past five years are suspicious."

Officer Bucks waved a dismissive hand. "Those were ruled accidents."

Tristan sat up. "I never believed Mike Riverton fell down a flight of stairs on his own. He was an expert mountain climber and very agile."

Chief Jones inclined his head in Tristan's direction. "As you've so vocally proclaimed since the day you arrived."

"And I know Brian Miller, who lost his family in a house fire, wouldn't have lit a candle in his home," Whitney Godwin said. "His death has never made any sense to me."

"Well," the chief said, "this will be your opportunity to dig into each death and prove once and for all whether Riverton's and Miller's deaths were indeed accidents or the result of foul play. The five of you will be assigned to Desert Valley until Veronica's murder, at the least, is solved. Then you'll receive your permanent assignments."

Shane let the chief's words about the murders sink in. Four deaths. Two unquestionably murder, and two suspicious accidents. Was this a pattern?

No. Veronica had simply been in the wrong place at the wrong time. In between a rampaging Tim and his sister. Veronica's death had nothing to do with the previous ones.

Desert Valley wasn't nearly the peaceful small town Shane had originally thought. It seemed death and danger hung over the sleepy community like a shroud.

Foreboding whispered across his nape, raising the fine hairs. Would someone in the room be the next victim? Or would Gina?

# SIX

Gina sat on the floor of the indoor training yard with a treat in her hand. The large space built with opaque skylights in deference to the Arizona sun was reserved for more advanced training of the K-9 officers and their handlers, but Gina hadn't wanted to go outside to the smaller puppy-training yard. Her palms had grown damp at the thought.

Not only would going outside leave her exposed, but the idea of once again seeing where Veronica had died left her queasy. She knew one day she'd have to face the training yard, but not today.

Sophie had understood when Gina told her she and the puppies would be staying inside. The ex-cop had offered to work in the arena rather than the office, but Gina had insisted she'd be okay. Just knowing Sophie was within screaming distance alleviated some anxiety.

Besides, the training center had two exits, one door leading to the fenced yard that was locked tight and the other only accessible from within the center. Still, she wished Shane were here with her.

For safety reasons. Not because she missed him.

Though she kind of did, if she were to be honest with herself. She missed the way he listened to her and made her feel special, cared for, even. It had been a long time since she'd felt either emotion.

Lucy sniffed Gina's closed fist, eager to get at the morsel of goodness inside. Ricky, on the other hand, wandered away, completely uninterested. That one was definitely going to be hard to train.

"Sit," Gina told Lucy while holding her closed fist to the dog's nose and moving her hand upward. Lucy's nose followed Gina's fist, tilting her head up while her hind end lowered to the ground. The second Lucy's behind made contact with the Astroturf covering the concrete floor, Gina released the treat. "Good *sit*."

Lucy gobbled the treat up.

After several more practice sits, Gina picked up Lucy for a quick snuggle. "You are a brilliant little pup. Now it's time to work with Ricky. Where's your brother?"

She set Lucy down. The puppy followed at her heels as she went in search of Ricky. No doubt Lucy smelled the treats stuffed into Gina's training pouch belted around her waist. She found Ricky in one of the agility tubes used during the K-9 training. The puppy had fallen asleep. She gently roused him. "Okay, Ricky, your turn to learn how to sit."

Ricky raised his head and quirked his ears, but not at her.

The sound of the interior door opening scraped across Gina's nerves. Her heart hammered a sporadic beat. She whipped around to face the threat and breathed in to prepare a scream.

Shane and Bella walked in. Shane held up his hands, palms out. "Whoa, it's just us."

Lucy trotted over to sniff Bella. Even Ricky emerged from his resting place. With a yip, the dog jumped from the agility tube and tumbled into a somersault before springing to his feet and racing to his sister's side.

Gina's shoulders sagged and she let out the breath trapped in her lungs. "I'm a bit jumpy."

He nodded. "Understandable."

Though a different sort of jittery feeling replaced the spurt of fear. She smoothed a hand over her hair, hoping she didn't look too messy.

She walked to Shane, and though her legs held her upright, they shook from the adrenaline rushing through her system. She hoped he didn't notice. And she told herself she was shaky because of fright, not because of Shane. "How did the meeting go?"

He lifted a shoulder in a half shrug. Bella lay down at their feet, and the puppies wandered off. "Okay. Last night's canvass of the area didn't turn up any witnesses to Veronica's murder, but the chief is sending Harmon back out. The Flagstaff crime scene techs didn't find any conclusive evidence to link your brother to Veronica's murder."

She frowned. "But we both know he's guilty, right?"

His grim expression didn't bode well. "Knowing it and proving it are two different things."

She blew out a breath. "Maybe when you capture him, he'll confess."

"That would be helpful." He rubbed a hand over his square jaw, drawing her gaze. Her fingers curled with the urge to touch the strong lines of his face. "No one has come forward with the puppy. Once word gets out that he's missing, hopefully that will spur some action."

She was anxious for little Marco to be found. It was so upsetting that someone hadn't already reported finding the stray pup. If someone had picked him up they might not know Marco had a home. "We should put up flyers. I took pictures of the puppies before giving them their shots yesterday."

"Good idea."

His approval warmed her cheeks.

"Your brother, however, is still in the wind and that bugs me." The grim look in his gaze spoke to his frustration. "The Mesa PD sent over a mug shot of him and we'll be out canvassing the town to see if anyone has seen him or knows where he's hiding."

Confused by his words, she asked, "But aren't

you and the other rookies leaving town for your assignments?"

Departments all across the state vied for the newly trained K-9 officers and their canine partners. Each K-9 team would go where their specialty was needed. Though Shane had said he'd requested to join the Flagstaff PD, where his family members served. For his sake, she hoped his dream came true.

"Not yet," he said, running a hand through his hair, making the spiky ends stand up a little taller. "Marian Foxcroft has been in contact with the mayor and the governor and talked them into signing off on her idea of keeping the five of us here. She has generously provided the necessary funds to employ all of us until Veronica's murder is solved—as long as it takes, apparently."

A flutter of delight tried to take flight but Gina quickly squelched its attempt. He was staying only long enough to solve Veronica's murder. Letting herself get all dreamy about him wasn't practical. Or smart. "I'm sure you'll be able to leave by the end of the week. Tim can't hide out for long."

His green eyes were troubled. "With the additional manpower, Mrs. Foxcroft has also requested that Melanie Hayes's murder be reopened and the suspicious deaths of two rookies be reexamined."

It took a moment for Gina to process the information. "I never met Ryder's wife. However, I did some training with Brian Miller and Mike Riverton. Their deaths were such a shock, but both were ruled accidental." Though her friend Whitney questioned the fire investigator's finding that there was no proof of foul play.

"Mrs. Foxcroft wants fresh eyes on the cases," Shane said.

"So you could be here for a while?" That giddy flutter resurfaced beneath her rib cage and this time it wouldn't be quieted. Shane would be in town for longer than expected. She wasn't sure what that would mean for her, but she had to admit she hoped to spend more time with him—as friends, of course—once Tim was caught and she could relax again.

Though a small voice whispered in her head, *To what end?*

The unspoken question smashed the flutter like a wet wool blanket. She didn't have an answer. Was there really anything wrong with some pleasant evenings? If they led to heartache, then yes, there was. As much as she longed for a family, she had to accept the reality that she couldn't, shouldn't, ever go down that road.

"Maybe. It could take time to satisfy Mrs. Foxcroft." Shane didn't look happy about being stuck here. "I'm sure my dad will push to have me released sooner."

"And that's what you want, right? To join the Flagstaff PD," she blurted, even though he'd already made it clear he was out of here as soon as possible.

A little V appeared between his eyebrows. "Yeah." Bella must have sensed a shift in her master, because she rose to all fours. However, her posture didn't raise any alarms. Her tail wagged.

Keeping her attention on Shane, Gina cocked her head. "That doesn't sound very convincing." Did he want to stay? Why? Her ego puffed up a bit in hopes his reluctance to leave was due to her. But that was ridiculous. She was silly for thinking there could be something between them. He'd never even hinted that he felt anything more than friendship and responsibility toward her. Which was just as well, considering she couldn't let herself seek more than a platonic relationship. Anything else would be unconscionable. Irresponsible even.

The emerald color of his eyes fascinated her. He was such a handsome man, but not in a pretty-boy way like some of those guys who graced magazine covers. No, Shane's good looks weren't classic, but rather made him more attractive because of the planes and angles to his face that weren't quite symmetrical.

Thick dark brows winged over almond-shaped eyes and added prominence to his cheekbones and a sturdy jaw. She forced herself to look away and concentrated on the dogs. The last thing she needed or wanted was to be entranced by this man even if he made her heart pound and her pulse jump.

"I'm more concerned about finding your brother at the moment than I am about returning to Flagstaff," he finally said.

His statement reminded her that he was here for the job, not her. Reining in her attraction to him, she offered a small smile. "And for that I am grateful."

"I'm going to head to the coroner's office to see what the autopsy revealed," he said. "Do you want to come with me?"

She shuddered. "No, thank you. I have no desire to lay eyes on Veronica's corpse again."

He inclined his head. "Got it. I'm more interested in learning if she was truly shot by a gun or a crossbow."

Gina's gaze snapped to his. "Last night you were sure it was a gunshot wound."

"After the attack on the truck, I'm not so sure. It was dark. The coroner will confirm one way or the other."

"You'll let me know what you discover?"

"Of course." Shane reached out to push a stray strand of her hair behind her ear. His finger grazed her skin and sent a quiver through her.

She couldn't remember the last time she'd felt such attraction. Discomfited by the contact, she stepped out of his reach.

His eyes were unreadable as he tucked his hands behind his back. "I saw Sophie on the way in.

She's trying to make some sense out of Veronica's bookkeeping."

"I don't envy her that," Gina replied with a dry chuckle. "Veronica had her own way of doing things and not all of them made sense."

He tilted his head to study her. "She was a tough boss for you."

Gina let out a wry scoff. "That's an understatement. I'm sorry she's dead, but I can't honestly say I'll miss her." As soon as the words left her mouth, guilt swamped her. "That's a horrible thing for me to say, isn't it?"

Shane shook his head. "No. You're being honest. Veronica had a very abrasive personality. I think she earned more enemies than friends."

Gina made a face. "That's true." In the early days, just after Gina had taken the job with the training center, she'd questioned her sanity for staying. Not just because of the genes that ran in her family line but because Veronica could be so nasty and mean. Who in their right mind would willingly accept her abuse? Right up to the day Veronica died, Gina had been butting heads with her.

Sometimes Gina wondered if Veronica had felt threatened by how easily Gina made friends with the other trainers and the rookies who had come and gone. "Has the chief mentioned a memorial service?"

"Not to me. Though he did mention Veronica has a brother in prison."

"I'd heard that, as well, but I've never met him. He was incarcerated just before I arrived in town."

"What about Veronica's ex-husband? You ever meet him?"

"I know of him," Gina admitted. "He's a doctor at the Desert Valley clinic. I've never met him. I do know there was no love lost between him and Veronica. I had the distinct impression there was some infidelity, but I couldn't say for sure or by whom."

He stroked his chin. "Interesting. I'm sure the chief has let the doctor know about Veronica's death."

Gina wondered if anyone besides the chief would mourn Veronica. She'd alienated most everyone in her life, though she'd never lacked for male company. She'd played loose and free with her love life.

Had Veronica thought she could charm Tim out of killing her? Gina's heart ached as once again the scene of how the event had transpired played through her mind. Even though Veronica had been mean-spirited and unkind at times, she hadn't deserved to die at Tim's hands. And Gina could do nothing to bring her back. "I should focus on the puppies."

"Right. I'll let Sophie know I'm leaving so she can stay alert."

The fact that he was taking her protection so personally sent pleasure through Gina. His concern for her well-being warmed her from the inside. "Thank you for keeping me up-to-date on the investigation."

"No problem." He smiled, flashing his white, even teeth. She felt the impact of his smile all the way to her toes as they curled inside her rubber-soled shoes.

"Come on, Bella," he said. "Time to go."

The puppies followed them to the door. Gina bent down to grab each pup by the collar until Shane shut the door behind him. Releasing them, Gina leaned her back against the wood for a moment. She'd better get a grip on herself. Crushing on Shane wouldn't do anyone, especially her, any good.

She glanced at the clock on the far wall. Nearly noon. Deciding she'd work with Ricky for a little bit before returning them both to their crates so she could eat lunch, she scooped him up and carried him to the cabinet in the corner where the training treats were kept. Lucy trotted along at her heels. Since Ricky apparently wasn't interested in the beef and sweet potatoes treat she'd used with Lucy, she'd let him pick his favorite.

Inside the cabinet were four bins filled with different flavors of treats. She set Ricky down and scooped up Lucy. Then, with her free hand, she took one of each flavor and set them on the floor in a line. Whichever one he gravitated to first would be the one she'd use.

The puppy ambled over to the treats and sniffed

each one. Apparently the little guy was a picky eater, unlike his sister, who squirmed to be released, no doubt wanting to get at all the treats.

Ricky stopped to lick one. Gina thought maybe they had a winner with the buffalo-flavored treat, but then he abandoned it to gobble up the one on the end.

"Ah, you're a fish lover." Gina picked up the dismissed treats in one hand before releasing Lucy.

Gina grabbed a handful of the salmon treats and waved her hands beneath the puppies' noses. "Come."

Then she walked toward the center of the arena with both dogs trailing behind her.

She stopped and turned her focus to Lucy. "Sit." The little pup sat, her sweet eyes expectant. "Good dog, sit." Gina fed one of the treats in her hand to Lucy then stuffed all but one into her pouch.

Ricky let out a protesting bark. Glad to have his attention, she held out her hand with the salmon-flavored morsel so he could smell the treat, and then slowly raised her hand as she'd done with Lucy.

Ricky, however, didn't cooperate. He backed up and barked.

Hmm. She plopped down on the ground and held out both hands in closed fists. One concealed a treat and the other was empty. "Which hand?"

Ricky barked and cocked his head.

"Which hand, Ricky?"

Ricky ventured closer and sniffed, then lifted a paw to scratch at the hand that held the treat. "Very good!" Delighted that he'd picked correctly, she slipped the treat into his mouth. It was a good sign that he could be taught to alert on a scent. He may prove to be a good tracker, cadaver dog or drug detector.

While he chewed, she stood and walked away a few feet, then filled one hand with another treat and held out her fists. "Which one?"

Ricky ran toward her.

The overhead lights went out, throwing the arena into murky gloom. The skylights allowed ambient light, but not enough to illuminate the cavernous arena.

Gina stilled. *It's just a shorted-out fuse.*

But deep down she didn't believe it. Terror flooded her veins.

A whisper of noise jolted through her. She ran and crouched down behind the agility tube. She grabbed treats from the pouch at her waist and held out her hands palms up, hoping to lure the puppies to her. Ricky found her right away. She clutched him to her chest. Where was Lucy?

A cold wet nose nudged her arm. With a dose of relief, Gina scooped up Lucy with her free arm. The two puppies squirmed and she stuffed treats in their mouths in the hope they wouldn't bark to be released.

Gina peered around the edge of the agility tunnel. The neon red glow of the exit light outlined the silhouette of a man standing in front of the closed door. Tall and slim. Unmistakable.

Tim.

She shuddered and jerked back out of sight. Her cell phone vibrated on her hip. She prayed Tim hadn't heard the muffled sound. She didn't dare answer. She'd have to release one of the dogs to get it and then the light from the display would pinpoint her location for Tim, ensuring that he found her.

Her breath came fast and shallow. Somehow, someway, Tim had located her whereabouts. How had he infiltrated the center? Shane and Sophie had made sure the place was locked up tight.

Oh, no! *Sophie!*

Gina's heart lurched. *Oh, Lord, please don't let Sophie be dead, too!*

As Shane walked down the sidewalk of Desert Valley's main street, he scanned the faces of the other pedestrians, searching for Tim Perry. Colorful awnings provided shade, though on this mild late-March day the sun's rays weren't blistering the way he knew they would be come summer.

Both sides of the road were dominated by storefront businesses, restaurants and hotels with stucco or brick facades. There was an eclectic mix of old-world charm and newer, modern architecture. Shane had heard that Marian Foxcroft had poured money into the town to bolster the economy as well as to entice more tourists to the small community.

Up ahead was the brick mortuary where the coroner, who was also the town's mortician, worked. As Shane reached the entrance his cell rang. He glanced at the caller ID. Sophie. With a spike in his pulse rate, he quickly answered, "Sophie?"

"Hey, so I somehow locked myself in the supply closet. I called Gina but she's not answering her cell."

He frowned, confused and alarmed. A twinge of constriction zinged through his chest. "Did she leave the center?"

Gina knew the seriousness of the situation. Why would she leave? Shane did an about-face and stalked back toward the training building, keeping his gaze alert for any sign of Gina or her brother.

"I'm sure it's nothing. Gina's phone is on silent since she's working with the puppies."

"Oh, okay." That made sense. Yet a large knot formed in his gut. He picked up his pace. "I'm almost there. How did you lock yourself inside the closet?"

"The door slammed shut. I'll have to check the springs on it."

That knot expanded and put pressure on his lungs. He worked to control his breathing. Doors didn't just slam shut on their own. Something was wrong. He sent up a plea that he reached Gina in time.

\* \* \*

Anxiety tightened Gina's muscles and full-blown panic built in her chest.

No! She couldn't panic. She had to stay calm if she hoped to survive.

She needed to reach the other exit, the one leading to the puppy yard. In a low crouch, she shuffled toward the agility tire jump, though the freestanding frame wouldn't provide much protection.

"Sissster." Tim's voice echoed off the walls. "I'mmm hhhheere."

Fear snaked down her spine. She struggled to keep hold of the puppies while she increased her pace. Thankfully neither dog made a sound. She'd sent up a fervent prayer for protection, promising she'd start going to church again, read her Bible and pray more if only God would make Tim go away.

Struggling to keep terror from overwhelming her, she forced herself to keep moving toward the exit. Afraid to let the puppies go, she had to juggle their weight while moving in a low run. She caught her elbow on the edge of the frame of a regulation jump and nearly lost her grip on the dogs.

Only a little farther.

The interior door of the arena banged open. The bright glow from a high-powered flashlight filled the space, forcing the shadows to abate enough that Gina was exposed. But so was Tim. A crossbow hung across his body and long bolts stuck out of a pouch on his back.

"Halt! Police!" Shane shouted.

Gina nearly cried with relief. How had he known to come back? God had answered her prayer. Though she couldn't see Shane behind the glare of the flashlight, his very presence made her knees weak. He was putting himself in harm's way.

Tim whirled to face Shane. He grabbed the crossbow, bringing it up as he reached over his shoulder for a steel-tipped bolt.

"No!" Gina screamed. "Shane, watch out!"

A whirr of movement caught Tim by surprise. Bella launched herself at him with a deep growl. Tim used the crossbow like a club to knock the attacking dog away. Bella yelped and fell in a heap at his feet. Tim turned and ran for the door at the back of the arena. Gina scuttled quickly out of his reach as he passed her.

Shane raced after him. "Stop or I'll shoot."

Not heeding the warning, Tim kicked the door open.

Gina held her breath as sunshine flooded the room, dispelling the gloom and washing Shane in a bright light. He had his service weapon aimed at her brother's retreating back. Her heart stalled. He pulled the trigger just as Tim disappeared through the exit. The bullet shattered the edge of the door frame and filled the arena with a deafening echo. Shane ran for the door and skidded to a halt, clearly debating giving chase.

Gina's stomach tensed with a more pressing question. "What about Sophie?"

A loud crash sounded from somewhere inside the training center, then Sophie ran into the arena, holding her gun in a two-handed grip. "I heard a gun go off. I finally managed to kick open the supply closet door."

What? Gina didn't understand—clearly her hearing was off from the retort of the gun.

Standing poised on the threshold of the exit, Shane glanced over his shoulder. "Stay with them," he instructed Sophie, and then he stormed out after Tim.

Gina released the puppies and rushed to where Bella lay on the ground. The dog's eyes were open and her breathing was labored. Tears filled Gina's eyes. She struggled to get her phone from her waist pouch. She dialed the police station. Though her ears hurt and the world was muffled, she managed to quickly tell the dispatcher what had happened, just in case Shane hadn't had a chance to before he came to her rescue.

Shane returned a moment later. "Tim got away." His grim tone echoed with anger and frustration. He knelt beside Bella. "You'll be okay, girl. You have to be okay." He bowed his head. "Please, God. Let her be okay."

# SEVEN

The acrid odor of burned gunpowder filled the arena. Shane barely noticed as worry chomped through him. Though he hadn't given Bella the command to attack, she'd done what she had been trained to do. And Tim had hit her pretty hard with the edge of his crossbow.

Shane's gut tightened. Too bad he hadn't aimed for Tim's back instead of firing a warning shot. By the time Shane had run out of the center, Tim had made it to the corner at the end of the road and disappeared. When Shane had reached the corner, there was no sign of the man.

On the way back to the center, Shane had had to use his inhaler. The first time in a long time.

Now he laid a hand on Bella. She lay on the floor panting. "You're a brave dog," he told her, hoping Bella understood how proud he was to call her partner.

Sophie tucked her weapon into her waistband at her back. Her training uniform was damp with sweat. Her honey-blond hair was no longer in a twist but hung in a braid, secured with an elastic rubber band. She touched Gina's shoulder. "Are you okay?"

Gina's slight smile showed appreciation for the other woman's concern. "I'm good. Shane returned just in time."

Sophie frowned. "What happened?"

"Tim. He somehow gained entrance to the center," Gina said. "He came after me but..."

"But?" Shane pinned her with his gaze.

Gina wrapped her arms around her middle. "He could have easily just killed me. Instead, he seemed more interested in terrorizing me."

Sophie knelt next to her and put an arm around her shoulders. "I'm glad he didn't hurt you. I'm so sorry I let my guard down."

"You did nothing wrong," Gina countered. "I'm just glad he didn't hurt you."

Unlike Veronica. Or Bella. Fury burned in Shane's abdomen. He looked at Sophie. "You being locked in the closet was no accident."

Sophie nodded. "So I'm gathering. When I heard the gunfire, I kicked the door down. I should have done that in the first place."

Chief Earl Jones barreled through the open exit. Right behind him came the town vet, Tanya Fowler, a medium-built woman with strawberry-blond hair and light blue eyes. Shane had met her the first week he'd been in town when she'd come to the training center to meet the dogs and their handlers. She'd been politely reserved with the handlers and gentle and loving with the animals.

Chief Jones skidded to a stop beside them. "Is anybody hurt?"

Shane quickly related the events while Tanya knelt down beside Bella and checked her vitals.

The chief called for Officer Harmon to come secure the scene. Then to Shane he said, "You'll need to come to the station and surrender your weapon and file a report."

Shane frowned. "Are you taking me off protection detail?"

Jones shook his head. "No. I want you to shadow Gina even more closely from now on. Your service weapon will be returned to you as soon as possible. No later than tomorrow morning. But protocol and policies need to be adhered to."

Shane understood. He knew the drill. He could remember days when his dad stayed home from the job because he'd discharged his weapon while on duty. His brothers had loved those days, but not Shane. Dad would regale them with horrible tales of the gritty side of law enforcement while devising some new exercise drill or obstacle course to put his sons through.

Mitchell and Jeremiah thrived on the challenge. Shane had wanted to earn his father's approval, too, but his asthma would knock him out of the competition quickly, much to the amusement of his elder siblings and his father's disdain. What would his father think to learn Shane had discharged his weapon and missed on purpose? Shooting a man in the back hadn't seemed right.

Jones turned his attention to the vet. "How is she?"

"Heart rate's up. Her pupils are slightly dilated." Tanya's light blue eyes sought Shane's. "Did she lose consciousness?"

"If so, only for a second," Gina interjected. "She went down hard. She's tried to get up, but she's obviously struggling."

Tanya nodded. "She probably has a mild concussion. I'd like to take her to the clinic for a full exam."

Shane lifted Bella into his arms. "I'll carry her over." He glanced at Gina, his chest tightening again. He didn't want to leave her unprotected. "You're coming with me."

She gestured to the puppies now rolling around together wrestling over a toy. "I better put them in their crates."

"I'll take care of them," Sophie said. "Once I get them settled down, I'm going to examine every inch of the center and figure out how your brother gained access and plug whatever hole he crawled through."

The fact that Tim Perry had somehow managed to breach the facility gnawed at Shane. He'd better step up his game. Maybe he wasn't cut out for police work, as his father had declared on more than one occasion. The fire inside of Shane burned a little hotter. He'd underestimated Tim's determination to get at his sister. It wouldn't happen again.

If Sophie hadn't had her phone at the time she was locked in the supply closet, it could have been Gina's body Shane was carrying out the door.

The thought made him break out in a cold sweat.

Gina stepped out into the mild late-afternoon sunshine that should have been enough to chase away her shivers. She was thankful for her sweater. The northern Arizona spring temperature was barely over sixty degrees. But her chill was more from her scare than the weather. She kept her gaze alert for any sign of Tim.

The chief insisted on keeping her on his left, using his big frame as a shield. Tanya hurried ahead to prepare an exam room for Bella while Shane carried his canine partner tenderly in his arms. It was clear how much the man cared for his partner. The bond that formed between canines and humans never ceased to amaze her.

A familiar yearning tugged at her. She wanted to have that kind of bond, wanted to find a man to love and who loved her. But fear kept the dream from becoming a reality.

Inside the clinic, the receptionist, an older woman with jet-black hair peppered with gray, rose and came around the desk. To Shane, she said, "Dr.

Fowler will meet you in exam room three." Turning to Gina and the chief, she held up a hand, stopping them from following. "You can wait out here."

For a moment Shane hesitated. Gina didn't have to be a mind reader to know he didn't want to leave her side. The thought both warmed and chilled her. The confusing reaction made her heart beat hard in her chest.

"I've got her," Jones said, clearly picking up on the same vibe as Gina.

Mollified, Shane nodded and followed the receptionist to the exam room. Once he and Bella disappeared, the older woman headed back to them. "Care for some coffee, Chief?"

"Thank you, Gladys." Jones tipped his chin to her. "Much appreciated."

Gladys sent Gina an inquiring look.

"No, thank you." She had enough acid reflux going on. Adding to it would only exacerbate the malady. She took deep, calming breaths and tried to block the terror that lingered in her veins.

Twenty minutes later, Shane and Bella walked out of the exam room followed by the vet. Delighted to see Bella up and about, Gina knelt to give the dog a hug.

Bella licked her face. Emotion clogged Gina's throat. She lifted her gaze to Shane. "She's all right?"

"She's tough," he said with obvious pride in his tone.

Tanya smiled. "She'll need to rest for a day but she'll be fine. I found no permanent damage."

Chief Jones's cell phone rang. He answered, listened and then said, "We'll be right over." When he hung up, he tipped his head toward the door. "We need to get to the station."

"Did someone capture Tim?" Gina asked.

Jones shook his head but didn't say anything more before striding toward the exit.

After thanking Tanya, they hurried to the station. Once there, the chief motioned for Shane and Bella to follow him. "Gina, you can wait in the break room."

Trying not to be hurt by the dismissal, she took a seat at one of the round tables in the space reserved for the officers' breaks. Her stomach growled, reminding her she hadn't eaten lunch. She'd left her purse at the center so she had no money to feed the vending machine. Instead she made a cup of tea from the communal box on the counter.

The rapid click of heels on the linoleum echoed in the stillness as Carrie Dunleavy entered the room and stopped abruptly when she saw Gina. Gina didn't know the police department's secretary well. In fact, she couldn't remember having a conversation with her that was more than a few sentences of polite chitchat.

Not in the mood to move beyond politeness right now, Gina smiled a greeting and resumed her seat at the table. She held the warm cup between her hands.

"I heard what happened to you," Carrie said as she glided forward, her brown eyes concerned behind the frames of her horn-rimmed glasses. "It's just awful. You must have been so scared."

Gina wasn't sure exactly what Carrie was referring to considering all that had happened in the past twenty-four hours. So she let her answer encompass all of it. "Yes, very scared."

"I heard Bella was hurt?"

"She'll be okay." Gina stared into her cup of Earl Grey as guilt for the dog's injuries choked her.

Carrie moved to the refrigerator and withdrew a white box. "I made cupcakes. Would you like one? Double chocolate."

Gina's mouth watered. Normally, she'd pass on sugary sweets, but today she'd make an exception. "Yes, please. That's so kind of you to offer."

Carrie used tongs to pluck a large cupcake from the box and put it on a napkin in front of Gina. The big round cupcake was encased in a flowery paper holder and the top was piled high with creamy chocolate frosting sprinkled with colorful confetti candy pieces. Gina bit into the confection. Rich, creamy, moist and oh, so delicious. She couldn't remember the last time she'd tasted anything this good. "Wow, this is fabulous."

"I love to bake," Carrie confessed with a shy, pleased smile. "It's my therapy."

Gina shot her a startled glance. Was she making fun of Gina? Did she know mental illness ran in her family? But Carrie's gaze held no laughter or mockery. Relaxing slightly, Gina remarked, "Probably more cost-effective than retail therapy."

Carrie laughed softly. "I'm definitely not much of a fashion horse."

"Me, neither. Dogs don't care what I wear as long as I have treats available."

"That's true."

Gina munched on the sweet in her hand, savoring every morsel. "I hear plans for the upcoming Canyon County Police Dance and Fundraiser are coming along nicely." A few ladies at the singles' potluck had been talking about the event held every year in May, though Gina hadn't been able to bring herself to attend. The event was too big with too much attention drawn to the attendees. She'd needed to stay out of the limelight, too afraid the publicity would attract her brother's attention.

So much for having to worry about that anymore.

Carrie shut the bakery box lid. "I'm on the food committee."

Wistfully watching the box of treats disappear back into the fridge, Gina remarked, "Makes sense for you to be on the food committee since you like to bake, right? I imagine everyone will want to taste whatever you make."

"Hope so. I should get back to my desk. See you later." She left the room as quickly as she'd entered.

Gina enjoyed the last bite of cupcake and washed it down with a swig of tea. Thinking about the upcoming dance made her wonder if Shane would still be in town come May. And if so, would he attend?

She couldn't stop the flurry of excitement tying her insides into knots. Maybe this year she would go. Maybe Shane would ask her to dance.

Her palms grew slick with anticipation. And worry. If he did ask, how in the world would she ever do the smart thing and say no?

Shane settled into a chair in the chief's office with Bella sitting at his feet. Chief Jones took his seat behind his desk. Ryder Hayes folded his frame into the seat next to Shane, his dog, Titus, moving stiffly to lie down next to Bella. The Lab nudged Bella with his nose, prompting Bella to also lie down. She set her chin on her paws.

The chief opened a folder. "The medical examiner in Flagstaff rushed Veronica's autopsy and faxed over the report confirming the cause of death as two gunshot wounds." He ran a finger down a page as he read. "Stippling at the entrance sites suggests the killer was within a foot of Veronica when the trigger was engaged. Two .45-caliber slugs were retrieved. The crime scene techs in Flagstaff ran the bullets through the National Integrated Ballistics Information Network but no hits."

Meaning the gun in question hadn't been previously used in a crime. At least not one that had been inputted into the database that the Bureau of Alcohol, Tobacco and Firearms maintained to provide federal, state and local partner agencies with an automated ballistic imaging system. NIBIN partners used the database to discover formerly impossible-to-identify links between firearms-related violent crimes and to identify firearm users or "trigger pullers."

"Fingerprints on the slugs?" Shane asked, thinking the perpetrator might have left behind a trace of evidence when loading the weapon.

"None viable. Nor on the casings recovered in the training center last night," the chief said. "I have Harmon and Marlton out searching every garbage can, crevice and potential dumping spot for the weapon."

The chief set the folder aside then pinned his gaze on Shane. "For the next twenty-four hours, you'll be relieved of duty while we investigate this morning's shooting."

Though he'd known this was coming, the order still rankled. "Yes, sir." Shane withdrew his sidearm and placed it on the desk.

"Ryder, take Donaldson to the training center. Find the spent bullet and casing. Make sure no innocent bystander was harmed because of Officer Weston's weapon."

Ryder stood. "Will do." Titus struggled to his feet, ready to work.

"And, Ryder, check in with Sophie. See if she

found out how Tim Perry gained entrance to the center." The chief steepled his fingers and rested his elbows on the desk. "Go over her alibi again."

For a moment Ryder hesitated, then nodded. "On it." He and his partner left the office.

Once the door closed behind them, Shane met the chief's gaze. "I'll take Gina back to the condo. She and Bella both could use some downtime."

"Good idea," the chief said. He reached for a paper on his desk and handed it to Shane. "Call the people on this list and check alibis. In some cases, double-check their alibis. If anyone seems the least bit fishy, flag them and we'll bring them in for a formal chat."

Glad to be of service, Shane took the list. A quick perusal showed the names of many people in town, including Veronica's ex-husband, and a few who'd left town, like Gina's friend Jenna Cruz, a former employee of the training center. He folded the paper and put it in his breast pocket. "Gina asked about a memorial service for Veronica."

Jones leaned back in his chair and scrubbed a hand over his unshaven jaw. "Arrangements will need to be made once the Flagstaff ME releases Veronica's body. I'll have Carrie talk with Randolph Drummond about a service."

"Has her next of kin been notified?"

"I'll drive out to the state prison and tell her brother, Lee." Jones heaved a heavy sigh.

Shane didn't envy the chief the task of notifying Lee Earnshaw of his sister's murder. Giving notifications was one of the harder parts of the job.

The quick rap of knuckles on the office door had the chief calling out, "Enter."

Officer Ken Bucks stuck his head in. "The rookies are all set up with desks."

The inflection in his tone when he said *rookies* set Shane's teeth on edge. It was clear the officer wasn't happy to be sharing space or duties with the newly graduated K-9 officers. Too bad. From what Shane could tell, the officers of Desert Valley needed help.

Jones inclined his head. "Thank you, Ken." Ken remained in the doorway. "Was there something else?"

Ken shrugged, not exactly eager to leave. "Nope." He backed away and clicked the door closed behind him.

The chief huffed out a breath. "That boy. Sometimes…"

Shane wouldn't qualify Ken Bucks as a boy. He was older than Shane by at least ten years. "Sir?"

"Sorry. Ken's my stepson. Ex-stepson, to be exact. I raised him through the teen years."

Shane hadn't known they were family. It was on the tip of his tongue to commiserate with the chief, but then he thought better of it. Time to change the subject before he said something he might regret. "Gina had the idea of putting up flyers for the missing puppy."

"Good idea." Jones's tone was rife with approval. "Have her give the information to Carrie to make the flyers. While they work on that you can file your report on the OIS."

Filing a detailed account of any officer-involved shooting was standard procedure. It would be Shane's first. He rose. "I'll do that."

He and Bella left the chief to find Gina in the break room. She sat at a round table by herself, staring into her cup. She'd retied her long red hair back into a neat braid that trailed down her back. Her T-shirt and light-colored cargo pants still looked fresh despite the trauma of her brother trapping her in the training arena. She looked up. Her pretty hazel eyes had lost some of the sparkle she'd had during his training sessions. He missed that sparkle. He'd liked that sparkle. He liked her.

"Everything okay?" she asked.

"Yes." He explained about his temporary leave of duty and that the chief had given him a list of potential suspects to contact. "He also suggested you work with Carrie, the police department secretary, to make flyers about Marco."

"Great." She pushed back her chair and rose. "I'll go find her now."

"I have to write up a report on the incident this morning. Then we can start hanging the flyers."

She touched his arm. "I'm sorry for all the trouble my brother has caused."

He covered her hand with his own. Her skin was

cool and yet warmth spread from the point of contact to the vicinity of his heart. "Stop that. Your brother's actions aren't your fault. He's chosen this destructive path. He's the only one to blame."

Her smile trembled. "You're a kind man, Shane Weston. I appreciate you and all you're doing for me."

Staring into her gold-flecked eyes, he found himself wanting more than her appreciation—he wanted her affection. Yearning pulled at him so strongly, like an invisible hook, dragging him toward her. The distance between them shortened as he leaned close. Her lips parted. She made a little noise in her throat.

His gaze jumped to hers. Was she distressed?

What was he thinking? Kissing Gina? So inappropriate, unprofessional and dumb. Stricken by his loss of self-control, he jerked back.

But Gina's hand fisted the front of his shirt and tugged him closer.

He'd mistaken her response as upset, but apparently it was consent. His pulse skittered.

Their lips touched. Hers were soft, pliant, and yet there was a hint of desperation in the kiss that made him want to weep for her. Gina was reacting to the danger and terror she'd suffered.

She was reaching out for contact as a way to assure herself she was whole and intact.

Shane's head knew this, but his heart cracked just a little as he disengaged. Reading more into the kiss than simple human need for connection would only hurt him, and her, in the end. A fate he hoped to avoid.

# EIGHT

Two hours later, Gina and Shane left the police station in his Jeep and headed for the center of town. From the back compartment that was separated by a tension gate, Bella moved from window to window, her vigilant gaze sweeping the main thoroughfare. Gina hoped the dog would alert on Tim long before either she or Shane saw him.

There was a measure of comfort in the dog's presence, but she knew they couldn't become complacent. Tim was out there somewhere and he wanted to hurt her, terrorize her and eventually kill her.

Gina was glad for a task to take her mind off her brother. She and Shane were armed with a stack of colored flyers displaying a cute picture and details about Marco as well as a plea to please contact the Canyon County Training Center or the Desert Valley Police Department with any information regarding the missing puppy. A staple gun and a roll of tape sat in the console between them.

Shane parked the vehicle so they could jump out and take the flyers into the businesses. He also had a photo of Gina's brother and showed it to every person they encountered.

Unfortunately, no recognized him.

Moving quickly, she and Shane managed to tape up flyers in most of the front windows of the businesses along Desert Valley Road while Whitney and James tackled the telephone poles and trees lining the street. By the time they were done, it was after five, and most of the citizens of Desert Valley were closing up shop and heading home for dinner with their families.

The setting sun painted streaks of vibrant yellows, oranges and pinks across the western sky, backlighting the dense forest of mesquite trees and ponderosa pines that surrounded the town. Normally, Gina would find the view calming, but her pulse still hadn't settled down to a regular rhythm after the brief kiss she'd shared with Shane.

She must've had a momentary flare of insanity, because she'd practically forced Shane to kiss her!

Okay, he'd leaned in, yes. But then he'd clearly reconsidered the wisdom of kissing her and started to back away. And she, well, she'd acted. Brazenly. Boldly. And so recklessly.

Though she regretted her impulsiveness, she didn't regret the moment. His kiss had poured through her like warm chocolate over ice cream, melting her all the way to her toes. That her legs had kept her upright was a surprise.

She'd never had a kiss so potent before.

Not that she'd done a lot of kissing. Kind of hard to find someone to kiss when she rarely went on a date, let alone allowed herself to become emotionally attached enough to warrant a kiss. Because she was too afraid to fall in love, to believe she could have a normal, happy life.

There'd been one guy before she had been forced to flee Mesa to hide from her brother. She'd met Roger Clay at a dog-training facility.

Both he and the rottweiler he'd brought in for training had taken a shine to her, making her feel special. Roger had been kind and caring, funny even. They'd gone out three times. He'd kissed her on their last date and she'd been left feeling let down and disappointed by the lack of chemistry.

Not so with Shane's kiss. The second their lips touched, energy flowed between them, thrilling in its intensity. But then he'd pulled away, leaving her wanting more.

She was in so much trouble. It had to be the stress of Veronica's murder, the missing puppy and her brother stalking her. Letting her attraction to Shane rule her head wasn't a good idea. She needed to keep him at an emotional distance. She could be friendly but professional. Yes, that sounded like a good plan.

Then why did she feel so out of sorts?

"It'll be dark soon," Shane commented. "We should head to the condo. I'm starved. We have steaks I can grill."

"Food would be good." Though she wondered if she'd be able to eat with her nerves jumping. Every time he got close, agitated butterflies took flight in her tummy and her lips ached for attention. "I need to stop at the training center to get the puppies. I don't want to leave them there alone all night."

"Of course."

As they approached the center, Gina glanced down the side street to her little house at the far end of the road. She sighed and wished she could go home. She had no idea if or when that would happen. It wasn't that she was ungrateful to Shane and James for letting her share the condo, but her house had been her sanctuary. Only, now it wasn't. Tim had violated her home and forced her out.

A horn beeped, drawing her focus to the Desert Valley Police Department vehicle. Chief Jones sat at the wheel. He rolled down his window. Gina did the same.

"I'm heading to the state penitentiary to talk to Lee Earnshaw."

Gina winced with sympathy for Veronica's brother. Gina knew Veronica and her brother hadn't been close, but they had been family. Gina imagined Lee would be angry and hurt by the loss of his sister. It was kind of the chief to drive out there himself rather than rely on the prison warden to inform Lee of his sister's demise.

"Stay safe, sir," she said. Desert roads could be treacherous at night.

The chief regarded her with kindness. "You, too, young lady. Stick close to Weston, and if either of you need anything, call Hayes. I left him in charge."

Shane leaned farther across her toward the window to say, "Will do, Chief."

Every point of contact on her body felt like a live wire. Electrical impulses zinged through her blood. His musky scent was a heady mixture and made her feel weak-kneed. She was glad she was seated or she might have had trouble staying upright.

With a nod, the chief drove away.

Shane slowly resumed his position in the driver's seat and proceeded toward the training center.

As darkness descended, the temperature plummeted. Nighttime in the desert, especially in the northern part of the state, usually came with a drastic change in temperature. At least that was how she attributed her sudden lack of warmth. Certainly it wasn't from missing contact with Shane.

As they rolled past the closed gate where Gina had found Veronica's body, Gina couldn't help but stare. Crime scene tape blocked access to the center through the puppy-training yard. The gruesome reminder had her bowing her head. She sent up a silent plea for understanding.

Why had Tim done this horrible thing? Why

was he so bent on killing his own sister? And why had he killed their father? Why had God made Tim with a mental illness?

But she knew she couldn't blame all of Tim's actions on his mental condition. Tim had free will, as did everyone. It saddened and sickened her that her brother chose to act with such malice and violence.

"Are you doing okay?"

Shane's softly asked question forced her to lift her chin. She didn't want him to see her as weak or overly emotional, even though he'd already seen her in a state of shock after she'd found Veronica and today cowering behind the agility equipment when he'd rescued her from whatever madness her brother had planned for her in the training center.

She wasn't sure why it was so important that she appear strong to Shane. Maybe if he believed she was strong, she could believe it herself? Believe she was strong enough to overcome the DNA flowing inside her.

"I'm good," she replied and started walking again. "We'll need to go around to the front entrance."

At the door to the training facility, Shane swiped his card over the reader and the lock popped open. Inside the building, lights blazed. Sophie stepped out of the men's restroom with a hammer and a bag of nails in her hands.

"Hey, I was going to call you," Sophie said. "I found how your brother entered the building. The lock on one of the men's bathroom windows was busted. I nailed all the windows shut. No one's getting in here again without permission."

"Thank you." Gina appreciated Sophie's take-charge attitude. "I'm going to take the puppies with me."

"Are you sure? Because I don't mind taking them home," Sophie said.

Gina felt a sense of responsibility to the puppies. And, if she were honest with herself, she needed the distraction and comfort of taking care of them. "I'd like to take them with me."

Sophie nodded with understanding. "They'll be in good hands, then."

As they were readying the pups to leave, Shane's cell phone rang.

He answered the call. "Weston."

Gina watched his face. He frowned, then his eyes widened with surprise.

"Where? We'll be right there."

He hung up but seemed lost in thought, his green eyes troubled.

"Shane, what is it?" Gina asked as worry flooded her system. Had her brother been apprehended? Was someone else hurt? Marco?

"That was Ryder," Shane said. "A maintenance man at the train depot found a gun in one of the trash bins."

"Put the puppies back in the crates," Sophie instructed, clearly excited at the prospect of finding the weapon that had killed their boss. Having once been a cop, she obviously still felt the thrill of discovery. "Let's go over there. I'll drive."

After recrating the puppies, Gina climbed in the backseat of the training center's SUV and wondered why Shane was so bothered by the development. He was quiet as Sophie drove toward the north side of town where passenger trains passed through on the way to their final destinations in midwest Illinois or Los Angeles.

The train depot housed not only the ticket booth for the passenger trains but the tourist visitor's center that Marian Foxcroft had insisted on building to supply the station with maps and town highlights. The building reminded Gina of a Tudor cottage more likely to be seen in an English countryside village than northwest Arizona. More of Marian Foxcroft's influence, no doubt.

Two official Desert Valley police cars waited with red and blue lights flashing, creating a strobe effect over the grim faces of the officers gathered on the platform.

Sophie brought the SUV to a halt. Shane shifted and turned to Gina. "You should stay here, out of sight."

She wanted to argue but knew he was right. Whatever was going on would provide a distraction that might allow her brother an opportunity to grab her or, worse yet, kill her. "Fine."

He and Sophie climbed out. Shane released

Bella and had the dog jump onto the back passenger seat with Gina. "Even though she's not 100 percent today, she'll protect you. I'd rather have Bella at 50 percent than not at all," he said before firmly shutting the door and walking toward the train platform.

Sophie electronically locked the vehicle doors, effectively trapping Gina inside the SUV.

Burying her hands into Bella's thick fur coat, Gina fought off the anxiety pulling at her mind.

At least she was safe.

But for how long?

As Shane approached Ryder and Officers Bucks and Harmon, the fine hairs at the back of his neck tingled. His gaze swept the area and though he saw no visible threat, that didn't mean there wasn't one.

He glanced back at the black SUV where Gina waited. He couldn't see her through the tinted windows but he imagined he felt her gaze on him as surely as he still felt her kiss on his lips. That had been unexpected. She'd surprised and pleased him when she'd followed through on what he'd decided was a bad idea. Not so bad at all.

Except he knew pursuing anything the least bit romantic with this woman would lead to potential hazards he'd rather not face. He may be sticking around Desert Valley for the foreseeable future, but that didn't mean he should toy with Gina's affections. Or leave either of them open to heartache when he eventually left.

Shane addressed Ryder. "Where is it?"

Ryder nudged his dog, Titus, and the two stepped aside to reveal a large plastic bag laid out on the platform. Resting in the middle of the bag was a handgun.

Not just any handgun.

A SIG-Sauer P220 fitted with a suppressor can. Exactly like the weapon Shane's grandfather had given Shane before he'd passed on. A weapon that was secured in a lockbox in the bedroom closet of the condo where Shane was staying.

How could there be two of the same weapon in Desert Valley?

Shane's grandfather had purchased the weapon new in the early 1970s when the Swiss company first produced the pistol for the Swiss army. It was one of a handful of sidearms that Grandfather Weston had bequeathed to his grandsons.

Shane lifted his gaze and met Ryder's. "That isn't mine."

Officer Ken Bucks snorted. "It sure looks like the one you were showing off at the church picnic a few weeks ago."

Shane wanted to wipe Bucks's smug expression on the ground. "Mine is locked up in the condo."

Ryder's expression held no hint of his thoughts. "I'll need to see it."

"Of course. I have nothing to hide," Shane said.

"Did you find prints on this one?" Sophie asked.

"It's been wiped clean," Ryder state flatly. "We'll have the crime lab in Flagstaff test fire it and compare the ballistics to the slugs taken from Veronica's body."

Shane understood what Ryder wasn't saying. If the two ballistics tests matched, then Shane could be facing a murder charge.

Concern darkened Sophie's eyes. "Who found the weapon?"

Ryder gestured to Officer Marlton, who was interviewing a man dressed in blue coveralls. Next to him was a pushcart filled with trash bags. "He said both the gun and the suppressor were lying on top of the garbage inside this can." He pointed to the nearest trash receptacle.

"Which suggests someone wanted the weapon found," Sophie said.

But why? Shane chewed on the question as acid burned in his gut. What purpose would framing him serve?

"Ken, bag the evidence," Ryder instructed. "You and Harmon drive it to Flagstaff. I've already been in touch with the techs. They're expecting it."

"Hey," Harmon protested. "Shouldn't we wait for the chief to give us instructions?"

Ryder's expression hardened. His blue eyes turned to ice. "I'm in charge until he returns."

Harmon shoved his hand into his pants pockets.

"Aw, man, Mary's not going to be happy if I'm not home tonight."

Shane didn't doubt that Eddie Harmon's spouse would be upset. With six kids at home, Shane couldn't imagine how the woman managed. He gave an involuntary shudder. It wasn't that Shane disliked children. They were fine at a distance. He had no experience with them and no desire to remedy that anytime in the distant future.

Once Bucks and Harmon left with the evidence, Shane and Sophie returned to the SUV. After securing Bella back in the safety of the crate, he slid back into the front seat. Gina's curious gaze bored into him. There was no help for it; he had to tell her what was happening.

"The janitor found a handgun in the trash can. A gun eerily similar to the one my grandfather left me upon his death."

"That's bizarre," Gina said. "I'm sure it will turn out that your grandfather's handgun is where you say it is and this is some strange coincidence."

"From your lips to God's ears," he said. But her belief in him warmed him almost as much as the kiss they'd shared. He hoped there would be more kisses. Whoa! What? Immediately, he pushed the thought away. No sense going down that rocky lane. Kisses, romance, emotions. He wasn't ready or willing to tread there. His career had to come first.

He sent up a silent plea that Gina's prediction

came true and this was all an uncanny coincidence. Problem was, Shane didn't believe in coincidence. Anxiety stiffened the muscles across his shoulders and up both sides of his neck. His jaw ached.

He forced himself to unclench his teeth as Sophie brought the vehicle to a halt outside the training center. Shane jumped out and opened Gina's door. She and Sophie hurried inside to get the puppies.

"Do you mind if I come along?" Sophie asked once they had the puppies in the back of Shane's Jeep with Bella.

"Not at all," Shane said though he was too pre-occupied by the turn of events to care about much at the moment.

Gina slipped into the Jeep's passenger seat while Sophie went back to the SUV to follow them.

"Don't worry." Gina laid a hand on his arm. Her touch was soft and comforting.

"That's like asking me to put toothpaste back in the tube," he stated. "Not going to happen."

They parked just as Ryder pulled up behind them. He climbed out of the car and grabbed a black bag from the back passenger seat.

Sophie stopped the SUV behind Ryder.

"What are you doing here?" Ryder asked with a scowl. "This is police business."

"Support," Sophie said and stepped past him to reach Gina's side.

Shane appreciated that Gina had a friend willing to incur Ryder's displeasure and not flinch.

Ryder shook his head and released Titus. Bella and Titus greeted each other before following their human partners to the condo. Once inside, Gina and Sophie took the puppies outside to the small backyard area.

Shane led Ryder to his room. "I haven't opened this side of the closet since before Veronica was killed."

He opened his closet and crouched down in front of the biometric handgun safe on the floor. Incredulous anger flared. Deep grooves marred the front panel and edges of the door where something sharp had been used in an effort to pry open the safe's door.

"Don't touch it," Ryder said, kneeling down next to Shane.

"The safe opens by my fingerprint," Shane told him.

Ryder pointed at the gouge marks. "How long have those been there?"

"Last time I used the safe was a week or so ago and those were definitely *not* there," Shane curtly informed the other officer. "But there's no way anyone breached the security lock. They'd have to have my fingerprint."

From the black bag, Ryder withdrew a fingerprint kit, complete with colored powder and various shapes and sizes of dusters. He went about the task of checking for prints on the outside of the safe. He checked all sides and found none. "Whoever attempted to break in wiped the safe down." He dusted inside the print scanner and with a piece of magnetic tape lifted one print. He scanned the print into a handheld computer device.

"It will be mine," Shane said.

"Let's see." Ryder held out a fingerprint inkpad and a three-by-five index card.

Shane pressed his finger to the inkpad and then onto the card. Ryder scanned Shane's print in, as well. The device beeped.

"A match to you," Ryder confirmed. "Go ahead and open the safe."

Shane stuck his finger into the slot and pressed down so that his fingertip flattened for the biometric reader. The locked popped open. With his breath trapped in his lungs, Shane swung open the lockbox door. Confidential papers, his passport and a hunting knife were the only contents.

His stomach dropped. Dread flooded his veins. "My grandfather's handgun is gone."

"It's gone?" Gina's incredulous voice came from the doorway.

Shane's gaze jerked to her. Her hazel eyes were wide with stunned disbelief. Beside Gina, Sophie stood quietly, taking in the scene.

"No, it's on its way to Flagstaff," Ryder amended. "Unless there are two of that make and model here in Desert Valley, which would be a huge coincidence." He gathered his supplies and rose.

Shane stood and squared his shoulders. His gaze held Gina's. "I didn't kill Veronica."

"Do you have an alibi?" Ryder asked.

"I was here with James until nine twenty." Which would have given him time enough to make it to the center and kill Veronica by nine forty, the estimated time of death. Acid burned in his gut. "Then I went for a walk."

"Did anyone see you?" Sophie asked, her tone hopeful.

Shane let out a relieved breath. "Yes. I saw a couple of home owners taking out their trash."

"I know you already surrendered your sidearm after today's discharge," Ryder said. "But until we can confirm your alibi, you'll need to stay away from the station."

His pronouncement grated on Shane's nerves. He hadn't intended to go to the station tomorrow. He'd planned to check the alibis of the people on the list the chief gave him from the training center. Even so, having Ryder say he wasn't allowed at the station, in front of Gina no less, made Shane's gut burn even worse.

"Could anyone else have opened the safe?" Gina's tone held a good dose of wariness. With the "evidence" at hand, he didn't blame her for doubting him. Especially after he'd practically accused her of Veronica's murder.

The dread in his veins bubbled hot when he realized whatever trust he and Gina had built in the past twenty-four hours had crumbled.

# NINE

Gina stared at the square safe on the floor of Shane's bedroom closet and wasn't sure what to think. Shane had been so certain his gun was locked up tight inside the metal box. He'd been wrong. Had he used it to kill Veronica? What possible motive could he have? And why would he then leave it somewhere it would be easily found? That scenario didn't make sense.

Shane wasn't a killer. He was a smart man who liked order and logic.

But more than that, he was a man of integrity. She was as sure of his honor as she was her own name. Shane wouldn't have killed Veronica. That was Tim's doing.

She lifted her eyes to Shane. The distress on his handsome face was real and assured her he wasn't being deceptive.

Yet, she couldn't shake the unease spreading through her despite her conviction that Tim was the killer.

Not Shane. Or anyone else.

But then who took Shane's handgun? And had it been used to kill Veronica? If so, how on earth had Tim gained control of it?

Shane held her gaze. "Apparently, someone accessed the condo while James and I were out."

"Everyone knows there's a spare door key in the police station," Sophie said.

Gina nodded, grasping on to that thought. "That's true. And I don't believe the locks have ever been changed. At least not in the two years I've been working at the training center with rookies who've lived here."

"Someone who has stayed in the condo before could have kept a copy of the key," Ryder said.

"That's a lot of people," Sophie remarked dryly.

"So a lot of people could have done this." Shane shook his head in puzzlement. "Though why would someone want to frame me? And how would some past rookie even know about my grandfather's handgun or this safe? And how could they get my fingerprint to open the safe?"

The questions hung in the air like dark clouds threatening thunder and lightning. Gina didn't have answers, and, apparently, neither did the others.

A sound in the front of the condo had Shane, Ryder and Sophie visibly tensing. Gina moved closer to Shane.

A moment later, James, his T-shirt and running shorts drenched from his run, halted in the doorway. He blinked at them, obviously noting their tension. His eyebrows rose as he scanned them. "What's up?"

Shane explained the situation.

James frowned. "You don't think I had anything to do with this, do you?"

There was a heartbeat of silence before Shane shook his head. "No, I don't."

James turned his gaze to Ryder and arched an eyebrow.

"I'm not ruling anyone out," Ryder replied.

Sophie made a disparaging sound in her throat. "That's apparent."

Ryder widened his stance and stared Sophie down. "Do you have a problem with the way I'm conducting this investigation?"

Gina hated how the situation was pitting them against each other. And from the manner in which Sophie squared her shoulders and met Ryder's glare with one of her own, Gina had no doubt things were only going to get worse.

"I don't like being repeatedly interrogated," Sophie ground out.

Needing to defuse the tension, Gina stepped forward. "This animosity isn't helping anyone. We know that my brother most likely killed Veronica and wants to harm me. He could have stolen the handgun hoping to get Shane into trouble. We know he was lurking outside the condo. I mean who else could it have been?"

Sophie cocked her head. "Well, there is the other murder to consider."

Ryder glanced at her sharply. "It's doubtful Melanie's murder is connected to Veronica's."

"Are you sure?" Sophie challenged. "I know you've been asked to reinvestigate her death as well as the other two rookies' accidents. And if those weren't accidents but murders…?"

"But the marks on the safe," Gina pointed out. "Tim could have succeeded in prying it open."

"Your logic is flawed." Shane's gentle tone inserted itself through the tension mounting in the room. "How would Tim even know about the gun? Even peeping through the curtains, there's no way he could have seen into the closet, let alone been able to get my print to open the safe. And we know he wasn't in Desert Valley when the other deaths happened, right?"

"No, he wasn't here. Tim was in Mesa when—" She faltered, not wanting to cause Ryder pain at the mention of his wife's murder. "The other incidents occurred."

"Time to change the door locks and maybe even add a dead bolt," James said. "The idea that anyone could come and go as they please creeps me out."

"I agree," Ryder said. "I'll have Carrie make the arrangements."

"I can take care of it," James offered.

"The department will pay for it," Ryder said. "But it will need a signed work order."

James shrugged. "Okay. Whatever you say— you're the boss."

"Only temporarily while the chief's away," Ryder reminded him. He walked out of the room. In a line, they followed him to the living room.

Bella, Titus and Hawk lay near the sliding glass door. Both puppies played with chew toys nearby. Gina wished she'd had a camera handy because the animals made a cute picture. That would be even better if little Marco were here to complete the trio. A deep hurt burned inside of her. Where was Marco? Why hadn't someone come forward with him? *Please, Lord, let the little puppy be alive and safe somewhere.*

Ryder whistled. Titus struggled to his feet and trotted to Ryder's side. Once again Gina noticed Titus's odd gait. She exchanged a concerned glance with Sophie. Ryder may not want to acknowledge that Titus was getting on in years, but the dog definitely was having some hip trouble. Hip dysplasia wasn't uncommon in large-breed dogs. Now wasn't the time for her to discuss with Ryder the fact he would soon need a new partner.

Bella and Hawk stood, their gazes trained on their respective partners, as if waiting for the call to action. Gina was gratified to see both Shane and James use the training technique she'd taught them as each gave the hand motion that let the dogs know they weren't going to work.

It was the same hand motion that Veronica had objected to. She'd thought the signal would be too confusing for the dogs and the handlers because it closely mimicked the halt command and the separate lie-down command.

However, Gina didn't think combining the two signals with an added motion was confusing, and obviously the dogs and their partners didn't either.

With his hand on the doorknob, Ryder said, "Shane, I'll follow up on your alibi. Then we'll talk again." His gaze swept over the rest of them, lingered a moment on Sophie, and then he gave a slight nod before leaving the condo.

Sophie blew out a breath that sounded full of frustration. Gina refused to believe Ryder thought Sophie had anything to do with Veronica's death. Though Sophie did benefit with Veronica gone, since the chief had appointed Sophie as the lead trainer.

The position came with the use of the training center's SUV and an apartment above the facility, which Sophie didn't need since she had her own place.

However, she had no hesitation about the SUV and had started it using the morning after Veronica's murder. Though the thought of Sophie being a suspect didn't settle well with Gina. She refused to think badly of her friend. Tim had killed Veronica. There was no other explanation that made any sense.

"I should go, as well." Sophie touched Gina's arm. "You have my number. Call me if you need anything."

Grateful for her friendship, Gina nodded. "Thank you, Sophie. I will."

Left alone with Shane and James, Gina sought something to neutralize the strain filling the air. "You said something about steaks?"

Shane ran a hand through his hair. "Yes. I did."

"I'm going to the store," James announced "Do either of you need anything?"

"The makings for a salad," she said, thinking they needed something besides protein for dinner. "I'll get some cash."

James held up a hand. "I've got it." He whistled for Hawk and the two left the condo.

Shane moved to the kitchen to prep the steaks. Gina hesitated, torn between retreating to her room and wanting to be with Shane. She could only imagine the blow it must be to think someone had used his grandfather's handgun to kill Veronica.

Until the ballistics test proved conclusively that was indeed the case, Gina would keep hoping for the best.

However, the need to comfort Shane moved

through her in a strong wave, and she found herself wanting to ease his worries.

But did she really want to get too involved with him?

Who was she kidding? She was already involved. He was her guardian protector until Tim was caught. And they'd kissed. Not that kissing signified a deeper connection, but whether she wanted to admit it or not, her heart was caught up with Shane. That was pretty involved, right?

She had to remember not to let things between Shane and her become personal. Or do anything that would lead to more kissing, no matter how much she'd enjoyed the one they'd shared. She knew he was only temporarily in her life. Once the cases were solved, he'd leave. Shaking her head at her preposterous thoughts, she pivoted and went in search of the pups.

After making sure they had sufficient water and food, Gina stepped into the kitchen, determined not to let Shane affect her. They were living in the same domicile for the moment; she had to overcome her awkwardness. Shane stood with his hands gripping the edge of the sink, his head bowed and his lips silently moving.

No doubt praying. Empathy swamped her. She hated seeing him so vulnerable. She started to back away but he lifted his head and turned toward her.

Reminding herself she had to keep things impersonal, she asked, "Can I help?"

Assisting him with something in the kitchen would distract her. After a beat of time, her words' double meaning made her press her lips together as heat spread up her neck and into her cheeks. She'd meant with the food, not with his emotional struggle. But to point that out would make too big a deal out of it, not to mention would be embarrassing.

His jaw tightened. The desolate expression in his green eyes tugged at her heart. She clasped her hands together to keep from reaching out to offer comfort.

He shook his head and pushed away from the counter. "Not much to do. I have the steaks marinating. I'll get the barbecue fired up."

He brushed past her, the air swirling with the force of his masculinity. He towered over her, yet she never felt intimidated by his size. Comforted, that's what she felt. Comfort and safety. Which were good, considering she was putting her life in his care.

She followed him to the patio with the puppies at her heels. Her gaze swept over the yard. The grass was dry and brittle but short, as if someone had recently mowed. James, she thought, since she and Shane hadn't been apart much all day.

Well, except for when she was in the training center and he'd been in a meeting with the other officers. She'd noticed earlier when she'd let the puppies out that one of the planks in the fence had been replaced with a newer one and nailed tightly down. Shane had said that whoever had been spying on them had broken one of the boards loose. She hoped the fix prevented any more unwanted visitors.

From her place at the counter, she could see Shane preparing the grill. His body language was anything but relaxed. His wide shoulders were hiked up and the muscles in his back bunched beneath his shirt. His movements were jerky as if he was struggling to go through the motions. Seeing his obvious upset overwhelmed her with the desire to ease his suffering. Her defenses were wobbling. One strong blow would bring them down for good.

But even if she could make him feel better, if she could rewind time and banish the situation, doing so would only leave her exposed and vulnerable.

She had to dig deep for the strength to resist the powerful draw she felt for Shane. Or they would both end up hurt in more ways than she wanted to think about.

After dinner, with Gina secured in her bedroom and Bella lying at the foot of her bed, Shane and James agreed to take turns on guard duty in case Tim Perry showed up at the condo.

James took the first shift. Shane tried to rest on his own bed though he remained fully dressed, but his mind wouldn't cooperate. Too many scenarios played in his head. Ones where he was charged and found guilty of a crime he hadn't committed. But the worst were of failing Gina.

When he did finally drift off, his nightmares were filled with him being unable to protect her. Tim dragged her away. Terror contorted her face as she reached out to Shane and called his name.

Shane jerked awake, drenched in sweat, adrenaline fueling his fear as if he were still within the dream. But the cacophony of chaos assaulting his senses revealed his nightmares had followed him into reality.

Dogs barked. Glass shattered. Gina screamed his name.

James shouted, "Halt, police." This was followed by the sound of an engine roaring to life and tires screeching on pavement.

Heart pumping with panic, Shane jumped up and raced out of his room. He kicked open Gina's bedroom door. The sight that met him squeezed the air from his lungs.

Her room was on fire. Or rather her bed. Three arrows pierced the thick bedding and flames licked at the comforter, threatening to engulf the whole room if Shane didn't put them out quick. Smoke and ash filled the room along with a sugary sweet scent that was out of place.

Gina struggled to free the puppies from their crates. Her long red hair flowed down the back of her pink robe. Her bare feet stuck out beneath.

Shane let out a relieved breath to see her unharmed. But he needed to put out the fire. He grabbed a decorative blanket Gina used as a throw from the back of the corner chair and beat at the flames.

One of the puppies got loose. Bella grabbed the pup by the scruff of the neck and carried him out while Gina hugged the other pup to her chest. For a moment she stood still, her gaze fixated on the flames.

"Get out of here!" Shane shouted.

She turned and fled. A moment later James ran into the room with a fire extinguisher. He sprayed the remaining embers with white foam. Smoke billowed out of the broken window.

Once the flames were completely out, Shane inspected the bolts. Two had the remnants of steel scrubbing pads wrapped around the tips. The third arrow, not a bolt, had a charred, gooey substance melted on its end and on the bedcover.

"There were two perps," James informed him. "They got away in a car a block down the street. I didn't get a good look at them or the vehicle. They'd broken out the street lamp."

"It had to be Tim Perry and he's got himself a buddy," Shane said. He touched the sticky mess on the bed and brought a sample to his nose. "What in the world? Marshmallow?"

"I know, right? The exterior wall took two marshmallow hits," James said.

"Can you call this in?" Shane asked. "I'm going

to check on Gina." He found her in the living room, hunkered down on the floor in front of the couch with Bella and the puppies. He crouched down beside her. "We put the fire out. It's okay."

She lifted her gaze. Her eyes were wide and her pupils large. "Tim tried to burn me alive."

Shane gathered her in his arms. "But he didn't. No Gina flambé today. Though the marshmallows were a nice touch."

She slapped at his arm with a snort. "Thanks a lot."

"Hey, it could have been worse."

She trembled in his arms. "The first arrow broke through the glass and landed near my feet and woke me. I jumped out of bed before the other two arrows came through the broken window."

He hated to think what would have happened had the bolts found their target. He kissed Gina's hair. He was grateful she was alive and uninjured. But it could have gone so wrong. He banished the terror from his nightmares turned reality and vowed he would not fail Gina. Her brother would not succeed in hurting her, not on his watch.

The next morning Shane and Bella escorted Gina to the training center. They were both exhausted. Neither had slept after the flaming arrows. They'd disposed of the burned bedding and mattress after Ryder and Harmon had collected and bagged the arrows. The chief surmised that Tim had used a battery attached to his bow to ignite the steel scrubbing pads. No one had any answers as to why Tim and his cohort had shot burning marshmallows at the house.

First thing that morning, Shane had Carrie, the station secretary, order a new mattress and bedding for the condo. Now Shane carried with him the list of potential suspects in Veronica's murder that he needed to call, since yesterday's efforts had been a bust. Not that he thought anyone but Tim Perry was the culprit. Still, he'd been given a job to do. The few people he'd been able to get ahold of yesterday had alibis, which he verified. But no one had been overly upset about Veronica's death. How sad was that?

Granted, he didn't get along great with his family due to his inability to fit into their idea of the perfect path a lawman should take. Still, he hoped he'd be mourned a little more deeply when his time came.

He planned to work inside the training center while Gina did her thing with the puppies. That way he and Bella could keep her under their watchful eyes. There was still no clue about Marco's whereabouts, and he knew the fate of the missing puppy weighed heavily on Gina. On all of them. He sent up a quick prayer for the pup's safety.

Sitting on a bleacher near the door where he had an unobstructed view of her and the two high-spirited puppies, he used his cell phone to make calls.

The first name on his list he'd been unable to reach yesterday was Dr. Pennington, Veronica's ex-husband.

The chief had already conversed with the man, but wanted Shane to follow up to see if there was any change in the doctor's alibi.

In most murder cases the spouse, or ex-spouse as in this case, was first on the list of suspects. Despite believing Tim Perry was the murderer, the police department had to do due diligence.

Shane watched Gina work while the phone rang. She had such a lovely and lively face. She was more relaxed when she was with the puppies. More like she'd been in their training class.

Today she wore a kelly green long-sleeve top with tan-colored pants. Her long red curls were tamed back with a ribbon. He liked it when she let her hair hang loose about her shoulders. It looked so soft. He tightened his hand on the phone, fighting the urge to go to her and release the ribbon.

"Hello?" The deep male voice boomed in Shane's ear.

Shaking his head to clear his focus, Shane asked, "Is this Dr. Pennington?"

"Yes, it is. Who is this? I don't usually receive calls on this line."

"This is Officer Shane Weston with the Desert Valley police," Shane began. "We—"

"I've already talked to Chief Jones," the doctor

stated firmly. "I have an alibi for the time of Veronica's death that Jones was supposed to substantiate."

Shane looked at the chief's note. "Yes, I see that you were in the emergency room at the Canyon County Medical Center at the time of Veronica's murder, and a nurse and another doctor have corroborated your story."

The doctor certainly didn't seem too upset by his ex's death. He could have hired someone to kill Veronica. But that didn't explain Shane's missing gun. He prayed it wasn't the one used to murder Veronica.

"It's not a story, it's the truth." The doctor's voice shook with rage. "Clearly, I need to speak with the chief."

"You could do that, sir, but he's awfully busy solving a murder. Your ex-wife's," Shane added. "We will leave no rock unturned in our investigation."

Dr. Pennington sniffed. "Well, I'm sure you'll be turning over many rocks and uncovering many lizards in Veronica's past. But I wasn't involved and would appreciate if you'd leave me alone." The doctor hung up.

Shane put a check mark beside Pennington's name. The next couple of calls were to Veronica's hairdresser and her dentist. Both had alibis, which Shane verified, and both at least had expressed some sympathy for the deceased.

"Hey," Gina said when she came over to sit beside him. "I completely forgot that I have a commitment this afternoon at the library."

Shane tensed. "Cancel."

"I knew that was going to be your reaction." Her hazel eyes took on a determined gleam. "You told me not to let my brother have power over me. If I cancel, then I'm giving Tim power over my life by flaking out on my commitment."

Not liking to have his words come back to bite him, Shane pinched the bridge of his nose. He appreciated and admired her desire to fulfill her commitments. But... "What is it you have to do?"

"Today is story time in the children's wing of the library."

He tucked his chin in confusion. "And you want to go listen to fairy tales?"

She laughed. "No, silly. I read the stories to the kids. I've been doing it every week since I arrived in town. It's my way of giving back to the community."

He hadn't known she did that. Knowing her wish for a family, her time with the kids must be precious to her. His respect and admiration for her increased. But he couldn't allow it.

"Take today off," Shane said. "You don't want to put all those kids in jeopardy."

A little V appeared between her brows. "Of course not."

"There you go."

The sparkle in her eyes dimmed. She scratched

Bella behind the ears. The dog nearly climbed in her lap.

"You're right, of course. I want this to end. I want Tim caught so I can resume my life."

He hated to see Gina's disappointment and could sympathize with her. No one like having their freedom restricted, especially when it was taken away in such a dramatic fashion. He wished there was a way to make her smile again. His gaze snagged on her lush lips. Smooth and soft. The remembered feel of them against his own mouth reared through his brain. Suddenly the collar of his shirt was too constricting. He gave it a good tug but that didn't alleviate his discomfort.

Her cell phone rang. She brightened as she glanced at the caller ID. "Whitney," she said aloud to him before she pressed answer. "Hi, Whitney." She listened for a moment then glanced at Shane. "I think so. Let me clear it with my shadow."

Shane made a face at her teasing jab, which elicited a smile, and the impact speared through him like a ray of sunshine, heating him from the inside out.

Covering the phone's mouthpiece with her hand, Gina explained, "Whitney has a meeting with the chief, and her babysitter is not feeling well. She'd like for me to watch Shelby for an hour or so. That okay with you?"

He appreciated her asking and he knew she was chafing at having to ask permission for something that she'd normally agree to without any reservations. "We could meet her at the station and watch the baby there."

Gina gave a small roll of her eyes. "My shadow says we'll meet you at the station. I'll bring the puppies." Gina laughed at something Whitney said. "Okay. See you then." She hung up, tucked her phone away and then rubbed her hands together in apparent glee. "I get some baby time."

The sparkle in her eyes nearly undid him. His chest constricted. His breathing hitched, but the cause wasn't his asthma—it was the woman in front of him. She took his breath away.

He cleared his throat in an attempt to calm his racing pulse. "I'll call Ryder to let him know we're heading over."

"Great." She pirouetted away to herd the puppies out of the training room. "I'll ask Sophie if we can take the center's vehicle," she said over her shoulder.

He jumped to his feet and followed her while dialing the nonemergency number for the Desert Valley police station. He watched her coax the puppies into the crate with treats and then step into Sophie's office out of his line of sight. His breathing finally eased.

Carrie Dunleavy answered the station phone. Shane asked for Ryder.

"One moment, please," Carrie said and then music filled the line and tension flooded Shane.

A moment later Ryder was on the phone. "Weston, I was just about to call you. The Flagstaff crime scene techs will be doing the ballistics test today," Ryder informed him.

Shane's stomach dropped. If the ammo in his grandfather's handgun matched the .45 slugs taken out of Veronica's body... Acid burned beneath his breastbone. "How soon...?"

"They said they'd have results by this evening."

Shane clenched his jaw. It took effort to ask, "Were you able to confirm my alibi?"

"As a matter of fact, yes."

Shane rested a hand against the wall for support as relief rushed over him. He sent up a silent prayer of thanksgiving. "That's good. Gina and I are headed over to the station now. Whitney needs someone to watch her little girl while she meets with the chief."

"Ah. I'll see you soon then."

Shane hung up, feeling the weight on his shoulders lighten. Gina stepped out of Sophie's office.

Concern dimmed her smile. "Is everything okay?"

"Yes." He straightened and shoved his phone into his pocket. "My alibi checked out."

He needed to make sure she knew, though why it was important to him to dispel any doubts she might have about him was a mystery. He told himself it was because, as her protector, he needed her to trust him. And knowing he wasn't a viable suspect would go a long way toward building that trust again.

"I knew your alibi would prove you innocent," she stated with certainty, and stepped close to unexpectedly hug him.

His heart thumped as he slipped his arms around her. Holding her felt so right, so natural. The fresh floral scent of her shampoo teased his nose and her hair felt silky against his cheek. He didn't want to let her go, but he did. Stepping back, he shoved his hands into his pants pocket.

She ducked her head, but he noted the pink brightening her cheeks. She bent to scoop up the puppies and handed him one. The fluffy ball of fur licked his face before he could tuck the squirming bundle under his arm. Gina's laugh invaded his heart and stole his breath once again.

He had to concentrate to force his legs to move. He carried the puppy and followed Gina out of the building.

"Tim killed Veronica to get to me. You had nothing to do with her death." She placed her free hand on his arm. Her touch sent a ribbon of warmth curling through him.

He covered her hand with his own. Their fingers entwined. He lifted her knuckles to his lips. "Thank you for believing in me."

"Always." She sounded breathless.

Did he do that to her? He leaned closer, wanting, needing to kiss her. Her lips parted in silent invitation. His breath grew erratic as he slowly touched his lips to hers.

One of the puppies yelped, breaking the enthralling moment. He jerked back. She gave a nervous laugh and turned away. Disappointment fisted in his gut. He'd have liked to continue kissing her. Her lips were so soft and tasted like the cherry Chap-Stick she wore.

He helped secure the puppies in one crate then secured Bella in the second and tried to pick up the conversation where they'd veered off. "Though my alibi checked out I'm not in the clear yet. If my grandfather's gun was used to do the deed the chief would have to investigate whether I hired someone else to kill her."

She walked around to the passenger side and stopped to let him open the door. As she slid into the vehicle, she said, "Yeah, that's a sticky wicket, isn't it? But I know it will work out in the end. You'll be proven innocent."

"Yes, it is, and I pray you are right." Anger at whoever took his gun churned within him as his chest bound up, making his lungs feel too big. He paused, breathing in and out through his nose in an effort to regain some calm.

There wasn't anything he could do about the person who'd stolen his gun until they apprehended the culprit.

Giving the anger any room only set him up for more stress. He shut the passenger door and walked around to the driver's side. His gaze snagged on movement near the tree line. The vague shape of a person shifted in the shadows.

The instinct to give chase was strong. From the back compartment of the SUV, Bella let out a loud series of barks. Clearly, the dog had seen the same thing as Shane. But he had to fight the urge to release Bella and go after the person trying to hide in the trees. Keeping Gina safe was his priority.

He yanked open the driver's door. "Get down," he instructed Gina as he slid onto the seat, keeping his gaze trained on the dark woods. There. Yes. Someone was in the woods skulking around. He grabbed his cell and dialed 911.

The dispatcher answered. "What is your emergency?"

"This is Officer Weston. Requesting backup at the Canyon County Training Center. I may have spotted Tim Perry, suspect in a homicide case, in the woods behind the center."

"I'll send officers to your location."

# TEN

Gina hunkered down on the passenger side of the Canyon County Training Center's SUV. Her heart hammered against her ribs, creating a thunderous beat that banged through her body. Had Shane really spotted Tim? Would Tim show himself again so soon? Was her brother more bent on hurting her than concerned about being caught?

Beside her, Shane slid down, making himself less of a target. The thought of Tim shooting a crossbow bolt into the vehicle filled her with dread. She'd been spared the last time by the grace of God. The bolt hadn't pierced all the way through the back of the truck's cab and embedded itself in her flesh. Her muscles tensed and she fisted her hands.

*Please, Lord, have mercy on me. On Shane*, she silently pleaded with God. *Again*.

She remembered the promise she'd made to God when she'd been quivering with fear in the training center, sure that Tim would find and kill her. She'd promised she'd resume going to church, would study her Bible and spend time in prayer.

Shame washed over her. Not once since then had she thought about her promise. She didn't want to call on God only in times of distress. Where was her praise and thanksgiving when life wasn't fair or neat and tidy? Why did she wait to reach out to the Lord when her life was on the line? She was like David from the Bible. God constantly provided and protected David and yet his faith had been weak and he doubted God at every turn.

She vowed to keep her promise. She just needed to live long enough to do it.

Within moments, the screech of sirens announcing the arrival of the Desert Valley Police Department echoed through the SUV, stirring the puppies into a barking frenzy. She longed to comfort them. They were scared by the chaos. So was she.

"Stay out of sight," Shane advised before sliding out of the vehicle.

She couldn't stand not seeing what was happening. Mindful of Shane's warning, she inched up enough to peek over the top of the dash. Shane conversed with Officer Bucks and Officer Ryder Hayes. Sophie came out of the training center and joined them.

A second later, Ryder and his yellow Lab, Titus, hurried toward the woods with Bucks and Sophie trailing behind them. Gina noticed Titus's odd gait as if his hips were bothering him. Something she'd have to mention to the officer. It wouldn't be good for Titus or Ryder if the dog couldn't perform his duties because of his hips.

Shane returned to the SUV and slid down as best he could, despite the steering wheel in his way. "We'll sit tight while they secure the area. I doubt your brother stuck around, but Ryder wants to be sure."

Her legs were beginning to cramp and the door handle dug into her back. She wasn't sure how much longer she could stay crouched on the SUV's floor. She shifted, trying to find a more comfortable position.

At Shane's curious glance, she said, "I'm cramped and freaked-out and angry."

With a gentle hand, Shane smoothed back a chunk of her hair that had fallen over her eyes. Her skin tingled where his fingers lightly touched her forehead.

"It won't be much longer," he said. "I promise."

She wanted to believe him, though she knew he was referring to being trapped on the floor of the SUV. She wanted to believe the police would find and arrest Tim quickly. But so far he'd evaded capture. And as long as he was out there, she wasn't safe.

A knock on the window startled her. She let out a small yelp.

"It's Ryder," Shane said as he straightened and popped open the door.

Relieved, she crawled out from under the dash. Sophie went back inside the training center while Bucks leaned against the police-issue cruiser to wait for Ryder.

"Nothing," Ryder said. "Titus didn't alert on any scent either. And the ground's too dry for footprints. Are you sure you saw a person?"

"Someone was in the woods." There was no mistaking the frustration and disappointment in Shane's tone, because the same emotions choked Gina. "It had to be Tim Perry."

"If it was, he's gone now," Ryder stated.

A muscle in Shane's jaw flexed but he didn't respond. She was proud of Shane. No good would come from him arguing with Ryder. They were on the same side. She leaned toward the open driver's-side door to see Ryder. "Thank you, Ryder."

Ryder nodded at her. "No problem." He and Bucks left.

Shane slid back behind the wheel. "Sorry about that. I know what I saw."

She laid a hand on his arm to show her support. "I believe you."

The muscles of his forearm flexed as he gripped the steering wheel. "I'm not sure Ryder did."

"He has no reason to doubt you."

"Right." He started the SUV and she buckled up. As they drove through town toward the police station, Gina noted with gratefulness that the police presence didn't decrease. Ryder followed close behind in his vehicle.

"I'm a little on edge," Shane admitted.

Understatement. "Aren't we all? A lot is going on. Veronica's murder is hanging over all of us. Your grandfather's special handgun is in question and my brother could be lurking around any corner," she pointed out. "But I appreciate your diligence."

"Thanks." He sent her a smile full of gratitude that curled around her heart.

She lifted a shoulder, trying not to let on how much she cared about him. "It's true. I didn't even think to look at the forest. But it makes sense that Tim would use the cover of trees to hide in. It's been his thing for some time. He'd take refuge in the park after a particularly bad manic episode. Dad had tried to interest him in wilderness training, but Tim was more interested in archery. Hence the use of the crossbow. He traded up from the harmless target archery set Dad bought him to the very deadly weapon that has become so popular in recent years."

"The woods. I wonder if he's holed up in the Desert Pines campground."

"I doubt he'd be somewhere that public, but maybe."

"It's worth having the campground ranger take a look around. I'll ask Carrie to send the ranger Tim's photo."

"Good idea." She appreciated Shane's proactive way.

At the station, Shane backed into the parking stall near the side entrance. Gina put a harness around each pup and held tight to the leash as both sprinted for a patch of grass. Bella followed the puppies, herding them to keep them from straining at their leads. It was so sweet the way the older dog's natural instinct was to protect and guide the two younger canines.

Officer Louise Donaldson pushed open the door to the side entrance. Tall and solidly built, she wore her short-sleeved, navy-colored uniform, complete with utility belt.

A badge pinned over the left side of Louise's chest gleamed in the spring sun. Her short brown bobbed hair had streaks of silver that glinted in the sunlight. If not for the graying hair, Gina would believe Louise to be younger than her sixty-plus years.

"Hey, I was heading out on a coffee run," Louise said. "You two want anything?"

"I'm good," Shane replied.

Gina smiled at the older woman while coaxing the puppies to the entrance. "No, thank you. Do you know if Whitney has arrived yet?"

Louise shrugged. "Haven't a clue."

Gina managed to get both puppies to the door. Lucy sniffed at Louise's shoes while Ricky chased his tail, twisting the leash around Gina's hand.

Louise's gaze softened on the puppies. "They sure are cute. But I'm glad I'm not the one taking care of them. They seem like a lot of work."

Gina didn't mind the work. "They are well worth the time and energy."

"If you say so." Louise slipped past the dogs and headed toward town.

Once inside the police station, Gina and Shane found Whitney with her four-month-old, Shelby, already in the break room. A stroller was pushed into the corner with a bright pink diaper bag hanging from the handle.

Whitney bounced Shelby on her knees. The baby giggled. The sound rippled through Gina, making her heart ache for a child of her own to love.

"You both came," Whitney said as they entered the break room. "Thank you so much." Her gaze went to the puppies. "They are so cute!"

The curious puppies sniffed the floor at Whitney's feet where a blob of spit-up had fallen. Gina gently steered the puppies from the mess with the lure of a treat. She gave the hand motion for the pups to sit and was gratified when both obeyed. So smart.

Bella also sat and strained her nose forward. Gina rewarded all three with a treat. Ricky took it in his mouth then dropped it. His sister swooped in and gobbled it up.

The baby giggled at the dogs' antics.

"I'll clean that mess up before I head to my meeting." Whitney stood and handed Shane her baby.

The surprise on Shane's face made Gina's chest constrict. He held the squirming cherub by the torso and at arms' length as if he didn't quite know what to do with her. He obviously had little experience with babies. Whitney seemed not to notice his discomfort as she grabbed paper towels.

Shane's panicked gaze met Gina's. He extended the baby toward her. "Here."

Laughing, she used her free arm to secure Shelby close to her body while handing him the puppies' leashes.

His grateful smile devastated her senses. He gazed at her with tenderness in his eyes. "You're a natural with her."

A blush crept into her cheeks. "Thanks."

Whitney tossed the soiled paper towels into the garbage. "I so appreciate you two doing this for me. My regular babysitter, Marilyn, is sick and I want to protect Shelby from catching a bug."

"Not a problem," Gina took the seat Whitney had vacated. Settling Shelby on her lap with her back pressed against her abdomen, Gina felt a contentment she'd rarely experienced before. Motherhood was a concept that seemed so far out of her reach.

Whitney said to Gina, "I'll just be down the hall if you need anything." She kissed Shelby on the forehead before hurrying from the room.

"Can you check the stroller for a toy or a book?" Gina asked Shane.

He found a set of plastic keys and several board books. "Here you go."

As she took them from him, their fingers brushed. His skin was warm and the contact sent a charge of attraction zipping along her arm. Strange how even such a harmless touch from Shane could set her nerves on high alert. She'd never had that happen with anyone else.

Shane pulled a chair close and sat while he motioned for Bella to do the same. The puppies wandered within the limits of their leashes, which kept them from getting too far out of reach.

Taking one of the board books, her own childhood favorite, *Goodnight Moon*, Gina held it up for Shelby to see.

Focusing on the book, she began to read. Awareness of Shane watching her intently made her stumble over the words. A flutter of nerves hit her without warning. She had to stop herself from touching her hair to make sure she looked good.

Giving herself a mental shake, she stared at the page, but she couldn't remember if she'd read the page already or not.

As she tried to make sense of the words, her heart beat erratically. She chanced a quick peek at Shane. He raised his eyebrow slightly and smiled encouragingly. She couldn't stop her own smile. Man, oh, man. She'd never been self-conscious when she'd read to kids in the past. At the library there would be thirty or so children and parents attuned to her every word and not once had she'd lost her focus. But for some reason Shane messed with her ability to concentrate.

Clearing her throat, she flipped the page and forced Shane from her awareness, though every cell in her body was hypersensitive to his perusal.

She needed to get a grip. Now. Letting herself get all fluttery over Shane wasn't a smart idea. But she had a feeling that controlling her response to him was going to be about as easy as finding shade in the desert.

Nearly impossible.

Shane settled back in the hard plastic chair of the Desert Valley police station's break room with Bella and the puppies lying at his feet. The puppies fell asleep while Bella kept her alert gaze on Gina and the baby as if she, too, were fascinated with the pair. Shane couldn't take his eyes off Gina.

She looked so complete and natural with the baby on her lap. The little girl's chubby legs kicked in apparent joy as Gina read. Her voice was both alive and yet so soothing.

A strange yearning filled Shane as he drank in Gina. It wasn't anxiety, which usually brought on the feeling of constriction in his midsection. His inhaler wouldn't banish what was causing his insides to compress and expand. Affection bloomed within him. She really was a special lady.

He thought about her fear of becoming like her brother. Shane didn't know the physiological or the psychological implications of her twin's mental illness, but he couldn't see her ever making the choice to hurt another person.

She wasn't wired like that. Nurturing was in her nature, a part of her makeup. Despite whatever stray component of DNA that made Tim Perry the man he was, Gina hadn't been afflicted with it. She was good, kind and compassionate. It hurt Shane to think she didn't know that or believe it.

A foul odor filled the break room. Shane's gaze dropped immediately to the puppies, but both were curled up next to Bella fast asleep.

"It's Shelby," Gina said with a wry twist to her lips. "She's soiled her diaper. Can you grab her bag for me?"

"Of course." He jumped up and fetched the pink bag.

Gina pushed the baby into his hands so she could dig through the bag for a diaper, wipes and a changing cloth. His eyes watered at the baby's stench but the happy little girl didn't seem to notice the smell. She twisted her head to look at him with her bright green eyes. She babbled as her legs kicked. She really was a cutie.

After spreading out a padded changing cloth,

Gina took the baby from him and laid her on her back on the pad.

"Whew," he said. "That's toxic."

Gina's laugh curled around his heart. "Have you never changed a baby's diaper?"

"That would be a negative," he answered with a shudder, but he watched with fascination as Gina made quick work of the task.

"What a good baby you are," Gina crooned. "I love your bright green eyes." She cocked her head. "Hmm. They remind me of someone."

"Whitney?" Shane threw out. He couldn't remember what color the other rookies' eyes were.

"No," Gina said, her voice puzzled.

"The baby's daddy?"

Gina pursed her lips. "Whitney has never named the father as far as I know but…" She shrugged. "It's none of my business." She wrapped the soiled diaper in a plastic baggie. "Can you watch her while I dispose of this and wash my hands?"

"Uh, sure." His heart raced. "What do I do?"

"Pick her up and sit with her on your lap, like I was doing. You can do it, I have faith in you." She walked from the room, taking the dirty diaper with her.

Good thing someone had faith in him. He stared at the sweet child and shook his head. Taking care of a baby wasn't what he'd expected to be doing in Desert Valley. Nor had he expected to be assigned to protect such a caring and loving woman as Gina.

Feeling inept, he lifted the baby and held her at eye level. Shelby cooed little bubbles of spit that made him laugh. "Hello, Miss Shelby." He sat back in his chair and turned the baby to face outward, setting her on his lap and drawing her up against his chest. Warmth spread through him. This wasn't so bad. He held out the plastic ring of keys for her tiny hands to grasp. A nursery rhyme his mother used to sing to him and his brothers when they were kids played through his head.

He softly gave voice to the words.

He sensed Gina's gaze and looked up to see her standing in the doorway. Her hazel eyes were soft with tenderness and joy. She was so beautiful it made his chest ache. He was happy to see delight on her face rather than the fear he'd seen earlier. He never wanted her to fear again. But that wouldn't happen until Tim was apprehended. In the meantime, Shane would keep Gina safe. But would his heart stay as safe?

The next morning, Gina awoke to two whining puppies who needed to go outside. She slipped on a pair of sweatpants and a pullover hoodie sweatshirt and opened the bedroom door. The scent of rich coffee permeated the air. Shane was talking in an intense tone. She hesitated, not wanting to interrupt him, but before she could close the door the puppies raced down the hall. She hurried after them.

Shane stood in the kitchen, talking on his cell

phone. He had on drawstring cotton pants and a white T-shirt. His hair was a spiky mess and he needed a shave, but she thought he'd never looked better. Her pulse sped up and she quickly smoothed a hand over her own hair, wishing she'd taken a moment to run a brush through the thick strands.

Still on the phone, Shane reached the sliding door before she could and opened it. The puppies ran outside to the fenced yard. Bella, who'd been lying on the carpet in the living room, rose and followed the puppies into the backyard. He left the slider open so the dogs could enter when they wanted.

"Dad, I gotta go," Shane said into the phone. "Give Mom my love." He hung up and laid the phone on the counter. He closed his eyes for a moment as if in pain.

Concern lanced through her. "Everything okay?"

Shane opened his eyes and met her gaze. "Yes. That was my dad. He's not happy about my extended service here in Desert Valley. He's trying to pull strings to bring me to Flagstaff."

"Which is what you want, right?"

"I did." He frowned. "I do." He ran his hand through his tousled hair. "I don't know."

He'd been so sure during the training sessions. All he could talk about was joining the Flagstaff PD to serve under his father. What had changed? A little flutter of hope wanted to think maybe he didn't want to leave her. But she quickly shot that thought down. But they'd kissed. Twice. That had to mean he had feelings beyond obligation for her, right?

"I need coffee," he said, distracting her from her wayward thoughts. "Would you care for some?"

"Yes, please." She filled the dogs' bowls with food and set them out on the patio.

"Did you sleep okay?" he asked as she returned to the kitchen.

"I did, surprisingly," she answered. Though it had taken her a bit to fall asleep, once she had, she'd slept hard without dreaming. She took a seat on one of the bar stools. "Thank you again for helping me with Shelby yesterday. I think she was taken with you and Bella."

"And the puppies," Shane said with a smile as he grabbed two mugs from a cupboard.

"Yes, they were a hit."

"It was fun," he said in a tone that suggested he was surprised.

"You were good with her," she remarked.

One side of his mouth lifted in a self-effacing smile. "That was the most time I've ever spent with a baby."

"Really?" She wouldn't have guessed that. "You did a great job."

"Thanks. You were magnificent with her. A natural. I, on the other hand, felt very afraid I'd drop her."

"That's not unusual the first time you hold a

baby, but you get used to it. Don't sell yourself short," she said. "You handled Shelby beautifully. You'll make a great father one day." Her heart spasmed. But who would be his children's mother?

"Yeah, I don't think so."

She frowned. "You don't want a family?"

He paused. "Normally, that would be an automatic no. But now after taking care of Bella..." He shrugged. "Maybe." He poured coffee into a mug. "After watching you with the puppies and little Shelby, I know you'll make a great mother."

His words brought a pang to her heart. She wanted children, a family to call her own. But the risk of passing on the faulty DNA that afflicted her brother would prevent her from ever fulfilling that dream. Shane's words reverberated through her mind. *Stop being a martyr.*

She wasn't. She was being realistic.

"Remember that day last week at the training center when you and Whitney were talking about children? You want five kids, right?"

He'd overheard their conversation. Embarrassment rushed up her neck in a wave of heat. "Doesn't hurt to want." She slipped off the bar stool to grab the loaf of bread. "Toast?"

"So do you?"

"Want toast? Yes." She popped two slices into the toaster. "You?"

His look said he knew what she was doing and

wasn't going to let her get away with distracting him. "I mean do you want five kids?"

She settled back on the bar stool and set her elbow on the counter. Resting her chin in her hand, she sighed. "I don't think it's realistic of me to want kids of my own."

"Excuse me? Why would you say that?"

"Bad genes, remember?"

The toaster popped and he moved to retrieve the toast. As he buttered the slices, he said, "That sounds like a convenient excuse to me."

Irritated by his comment, she straightened. "It's a valid consideration."

"Maybe, maybe not."

"I told you, mental illness runs in my mother's family. I don't want to perpetuate it."

"You can't be sure you would."

"My mother's sister was also diagnosed with schizoaffective disorder. She was institutionalized when she was twenty-five. She killed herself on her thirtieth birthday."

"That's rough." Sympathy tinged the green in his eyes. "But your mother wasn't afflicted. Right? Heredity may be a factor, but fearing that something might happen when you really have no control over *if* something will happen is no way to live your life. I think this is where faith comes in. You need to believe God is in control."

She wanted to trust God, to let Him be in control of her life, but it was hard to do. The fear seemed too big, too overwhelming. How could faith banish the fear? A memory surfaced, long buried beneath the anguish and grief of losing her family. "'God has not given us a spirit of fear, but of power, of love, of a sound mind.'" She repeated the words she'd once heard her father recite to her mother.

"Exactly," Shane said with a pleased smile. "Second Timothy, chapter one, verse seven."

"You know your Bible."

He nodded. "Mom took us to church every Sunday, and summers there was vacation Bible school, then day camps and eventually overnight camps. Some far away. The best were the weeklong camps in the milder climate of South Lake Tahoe in the Sierra Nevada Mountains of California."

They'd had such different upbringings. "I volunteered at the animal shelter during school breaks, though we attended church on Sunday mornings as a family. I would have liked to go to the mountains. We didn't travel or even get out of the city much." She sighed. "I keep meaning to explore around here. Just haven't made time." Or felt like going alone. But she couldn't admit that to him.

He reached across the bar to take her hand. The warmth of his skin shot through her, making her overly hot.

"Once this is all over we can plan a day hike," he said. "We can take the dogs."

She blinked back sudden tears. She longed to

take him up on the offer. "That would be nice, if you're still in Desert Valley…"

"Good." Shane withdrew his hand, taking his warmth with him. She wrapped her hands around the full mug of coffee he'd set in front of her. He moved to the refrigerator and took out a carton of eggs. "Do you like your eggs scrambled or fried?"

"Whatever is easiest." She was unused to having someone cater to her needs. It felt strange to sit idle while he cooked.

Wanting to take the focus off her, she said, "You mentioned you have brothers. I didn't think to ask, are they younger than you?"

"No. They're older. Mitchell is thirty-five and Jeremiah is thirty-one. Both are single and both are on the job in Flagstaff."

"So you're the baby of the family."

"Yep. And a disappointment to my dad."

That was out of the blue. "What do you mean?"

He scrubbed a hand over his jaw. "Whoa, I can't believe I said that out loud."

"Why do you believe you're a disappointment?"

"Unlike the other men in my family, I didn't make it in the military."

That was surprising. "What happened?"

"Asthma."

"You have asthma?" She'd seen no indication of a breathing problem while working with him and Bella.

"I do. It flares up occasionally. Stress can trigger an attack and so can allergens. But the military won't take someone who's had an asthma diagnosis after the age of 13."

"I didn't know that. But asthma didn't prevent you from completing the police academy."

"No, it didn't. Thankfully." He set a plate of fluffy scrambled eggs in front of her.

"Your dad has to be proud of you for becoming a police officer like him," she reasoned.

He shrugged. "I suppose. Though he'd rather I went the traditional route of patrol, then detective. Being a K-9 officer wasn't what he had in mind."

"Did you always want to be in law enforcement?"

He shook his head. "No. When I was a kid I wanted to be a veterinarian."

"Really? Why didn't you become one?"

"Because I went the way of expectations. I wanted my family's approval. And their respect."

Her heart hurt to realize he wasn't living the life he wanted. "If you don't want to be a police officer then you shouldn't be. You need to find what makes you happy and not worry about what your family wants. They'll respect you for being your own person."

He paused, cocking his head to the side. "The strange thing is, I like police work and I want to excel at it. For me, not just for them."

That statement made her feel somewhat better. "You and Bella work well together."

"Thanks." He grinned. "We had great training."

She laughed, pleased by the compliment.

His cell phone vibrated against the counter, drawing not only their attention but Bella's, as well. She entered through the open slider with the puppies following closely behind. Gina liked how the older dog was teaching the younger ones. Bella sat at the ready as Shane answered the call.

"Weston."

He visibly tensed. "We're on our way." He signed off quickly. "That was the chief. Apparently someone has taken the clerk at the Sun Break minimart hostage. The perp fits the description of your brother."

Her breath caught. Oh, no. A hostage. *Please, Lord, don't let Tim hurt the person.*

Could they finally capture and arrest Tim? Would she finally be free of his threats? She slid off the stool. "I'll be ready in five."

He nodded. They both hurried to their respective rooms to change. The Sun Break was a small mom-and-pop convenience store on the outskirts of town. She sent up a plea that God wouldn't allow Tim to hurt anyone else the way he had Veronica. And that her brother would be caught once and for all.

# ELEVEN

Shane brought his vehicle to an abrupt halt at the perimeter of the barricade around the Sun Break minimart made by three Desert Valley police cruisers. Officers Harmon, Bucks and Marlton crouched behind the vehicles with their weapons aimed at the minimart's front door.

Chief Jones and Officer Ryder Hayes and his partner, Titus, were off to one side. Both men wore flak vests with the initials DVPD across the front and back. They had a blueprint of the store spread out on the back end of the Desert Valley K-9 Unit vehicle. Ryder had his cell phone to his ear.

"Stay here and lock the doors," Shane advised Gina. Since everyone had been called out, there was no one left at the station in a position to adequately protect her. He didn't want her in the line of fire. If Tim caught sight of her, he might take a shot at her.

"I might be able help," she countered. "Tim may let the hostages go in exchange for me."

"That's not happening," Shane practically growled as a tight fist of dread clasped his heart and squeezed. "There's no way I'm letting you sacrifice yourself. We'll get him out without anyone getting hurt."

"Though I love your optimism, you can't guarantee someone won't get hurt." She popped open her door. "I'd rather it not be an innocent bystander."

"Gina!" Shane made a grab for her, but she was too quick. She was out of the vehicle and hurrying toward the chief.

Infused with frustration, he exited the Jeep, briefly touching the butt of his sidearm, thankful the chief had released it back to him. He released Bella from the back, quickly leashing her before following Gina to where Chief Jones and Ryder stood. Shane was glad they'd taken the time to drop the puppies off with Sophie, though he could tell the ex-cop had wanted to ride along with them.

Chief Jones glanced their way. "He's barricaded the door. We've tried to reach him on the store's landline, but he won't answer. So we've resorted to the bullhorn." He held up the white horn.

Gina stepped up. "Chief, let me try to talk to him."

He handed her the horn. "It's worth a shot."

Her nerves shook, making her hand tremble as she held the bullhorn up to her mouth. "Tim, it's Gina. Please pick up the phone. I want to talk to you. I want to understand."

A face appeared in the window. A man or

woman? Shane's gut tightened. He remembered a hostage situation his father had once told him and his brothers about. A man had taken his neighbor's family hostage because he believed they'd talked the man's wife into leaving him.

And every time the hostage negotiator reached out to the kidnapper, a hostage was killed. Dad had finally ordered his men to breach the house, which resulted in the kidnapper's death but spared two children their parents' fate. Shane sent up a silent plea to God not to let this situation turn into a killing spree.

"Try the phone again," Jones instructed Ryder.

Ryder nodded and dialed. He put the call on speaker so the sound of the ringer echoed through the air. After a moment the line was picked up.

"What?" a deep voice demanded.

Gina frowned and met Shane's gaze. She whispered, "That's not Tim."

"Who am I speaking with?" the chief asked.

"I'm not talking to you," came the terse reply, though the words were slightly slurred. "I want to go home." The way he drew out the last word reminded Shane of a child having a tantrum.

"You want to go home. I can understand that," the chief said. "Where's home?"

"Santa Fe. I need money for the train to take me home. Nobody was supposed to get hurt."

Shane winced. That didn't sound promising.

"You want enough money to make it to Santa Fe.

Of course you didn't mean to hurt anyone." Sweat trickled down the chief's brow. He wiped the back of his hand across his forehead. "Could you let the injured leave? We can take care of them out here while we work on getting you home."

The chief impressed Shane. He was mirroring the kidnapper's words and showing empathy, which would hopefully go a long way toward building trust with the kidnapper.

"You'll help me?" Doubt echoed in the man's voice. "Robin Hood said I shouldn't believe anyone. He's coming back. He'll help me."

Shane shared a stunned glance with the others. A sinking feeling settled in the pit of his stomach. Was Robin Hood Tim Perry? Was this guy the same one who had been with Tim when he shot the flaming arrows into Gina's bedroom?

"Sure, we'll help you," the chief assured him. "There's a train bound for Santa Fe tonight. We could get you on it."

"No. You won't let me go," the kidnapper said. "Robin Hood said you'll hurt me if you catch me."

The chief put his hand over the phone's microphone and addressed Ryder. "You and Weston go around back. See if you can get in while I keep him occupied on the line."

Shane was pleased the chief trusted him with the assignment. But he didn't want to leave Gina. If Robin Hood was her brother, then according to the guy on the phone, he was coming back. Shane needed to be here to protect her.

She put her hand on his arm. "I'll stay right here with the chief. Be careful."

Touched by her concern and by the knowledge she'd known what he was thinking, he squeezed her hand. He met the chief's gaze. The older man nodded, a silent promise to protect Gina. Relinquishing control wasn't easy, but Shane knew he had to trust the chief to keep Gina safe. Urging Bella into action, they followed Ryder and Titus in a wide arc that took them behind the minimart.

At the back door, Ryder easily turned the knob and the door swung soundlessly open. Shane and Bella hung back, allowing the senior officer and his partner to enter first.

Nerves stretched taut, Shane stepped inside with Bella at his heels. The corridor took them past a small office space and stacks of inventory. They came to a set of swinging doors with square windows. Ryder pressed his back to one side of the door while Shane mirrored him on the other side. He peered through the window. Tall shelves full of packaged goods obscured the view.

Ryder eased open one side of the door and slipped into the store. Shane followed suit. Ryder gestured to Shane to approach the front from the left while Ryder would take the path to the right.

Though a bout of nervous anxiety zinged through Shane, he had trained for this—he knew what to do. He took a calming breath and set his mind to the task at hand. In a low crouch, he headed for the far left aisle and peered around the shelves. He had an unobstructed view of the cash register, where a thin man stood holding a sawed-off shotgun in one hand and the store's phone pressed against his ear with the other. Shane saw only the one kidnapper.

The man's slurred voice rose and fell in agitation. He shifted from foot to foot, clearly amped up. From adrenaline? Or were drugs involved?

Stringy brown hair spilled over the collar of a worn leather jacket. The jacket was too heavy for Arizona, even at this time of year. On the left shoulder, a patch snagged Shane's notice. A Native American symbol by his guess, but one he wasn't familiar with. A black arrow pointing upward with three black feathers at the bottom and beneath the arrow's tip was what looked like a skull. The man had said he was from New Mexico; perhaps the symbol had meaning in the other state.

A mirror above the man's head provided a panorama of the store and revealed Ryder and Titus herding a group of kids and a lady out the rear exit. Shane prayed the kidnapper didn't look up, but that was a risk they had to take to get the hostages out safely.

Shane hustled Bella across the aisle to another tall shelf, grimacing as her nails clicked on the linoleum floor. He peered around the corner along the refrigerated cases. A man and two teens huddled together in the middle of the aisle. Shane waved them toward him. The trio hurried to his side.

"Stay out of sight," Shane whispered.

The man nodded, putting his arms around the boys as they hunkered down at the end of the aisle.

Shane and Bella moved toward the front of the store. When they reached the end of the shelving rack, he chanced a peek at the kidnapper. The man cradled the phone against his shoulder and grabbed the store clerk, a middle-aged woman with a riot of black curls, by the back of her collar. He pressed her against the front window with the shotgun pointed at her head. The woman let out a terrified yelp.

It took everything in Shane not to rush to her aid. Not yet. If he moved too soon, it might spook the kidnapper and cost the woman her life. The priority was securing the clerk's safety. Shane said a quick prayer of protection and for success. In the mirror above the register, Shane saw Ryder and Titus return, along with Officer Bucks.

Catching Ryder's eye in the reflection, Shane pointed to himself then to the man holding the shotgun. Ryder nodded. Taking that to mean Shane was clear to make a move, he unleashed Bella and stepped from the aisle with his gun drawn. "Police! Drop your weapon!"

The kidnapper whirled toward Shane. A bag of marshmallows dropped from beneath his jacket. The store clerk lunged away. Bella sprinted forward and leaped at the man, latching on to his forearm, forcing him to relinquish his hold on the shotgun. It clattered to the floor.

With a scream, the kidnapper dropped the phone and pummeled Bella with his fist.

Titus's barks ricocheted off the linoleum floor as Ryder grabbed the man's flaying arm and bent it back behind him.

"Release," Shane instructed Bella. The dog immediately complied but kept her alert gaze on the suspect as Ryder subdued the man by pushing him to the floor and slapped cuffs on his wrists. Shane clicked the leash back on Bella once the man was secured. He toed the bag of marshmallows. Had they planned on more letting loose more flaming arrows?

The sales clerk sank to her knees in tears. Her name tag read Ronda.

Bucks and Ryder led the kidnapper out of the store. Shane and Bella helped the clerk to stand. "Are you hurt?"

She shook her head. "No. Scared. That man's crazy. I think he was high on something."

"There was another man with him," Shane said. "Where did he go?"

"He ran out as soon as he heard the sirens."

Frustrated disappointment camped out in his chest. He needed to get back to Gina.

Ronda scrunched up her nose. "They both smelled horrible. When they came up to the counter and demanded money, I thought I was going to gag from the stench."

"Was anyone else hurt?" Shane hadn't seen any injured hostages but he had to ask to be sure.

"No. That one kept waving that shotgun around but he never fired it," Ronda said. "Thankfully, we weren't too busy this morning."

"That is a blessing," Shane agreed. Though he doubted those who'd been trapped inside the store would define the situation in that way. The blessing was that no one was harmed. Shane escorted Ronda and the other customers out the front entrance. Officers Marlton and Harmon rushed forward to take the hostages' statements.

A crowd had gathered around the perimeter, and Shane sought Gina out. She stood where he'd left her by the chief's side, looking lovely with sunshine bathing her in a warm glow and making her red hair spark. He headed toward her with an urgency that confused him.

The relief in her eyes twisted him up inside.

She'd been really worried.

About him?

He was surprised by the ribbon of warmth twining through his chest.

She cared? It scared and pleased him at the same time. A romantic relationship with the lovely trainer wasn't in his future, yet there was a part of him that yearned to see where a romance with Gina could lead. Boy, he was in deep trouble.

The chief stepped into his path before he reached Gina's side. "Good job, Weston." The chief slapped him on the back.

"Thank you, sir. But Bella's to be commended. She disarmed him."

The chief nodded. "Of course. It's gratifying to see the Canyon County Training Center is so effective."

"It is, sir," Shane assured him. "Gina and Sophie are excellent at their jobs."

Chief Jones's gaze narrowed. "So was Veronica."

"She was, sir," he was quick to agree, though he hadn't technically worked with Veronica. She'd had a more hands-off approach, letting Gina and Sophie do the work and then taking the credit for herself. But Shane kept that quiet, not wanting to disparage Veronica to the chief. "Sir, the store clerk confirmed there was another man with our suspect, but he escaped before we arrived. I'm sure it was Tim Perry."

The chief ran a hand over his jaw. "Then we definitely need this suspect to talk. He may be the lead that breaks the case."

"Yes, sir." Shane hoped so.

After seating the suspect in the back of Bucks's cruiser and leaving Bucks to keep an eye on the man, Ryder and Titus walked over.

"Our guy's in bad shape," Ryder said. "High as a kite. Barely lucid. He's got track marks on both arms."

"Did he say anything more about Robin Hood?"

"Nothing useful. Just keeps blathering on about his merry band of men and that he was only allowed to shoot marshmallows."

Had Tim enlisted more than one junkie to help his cause? Shane had figured something like that. "Did you get an ID on him?"

"Yes, he's in the national criminal database. His name's John Krause, from Santa Fe, New Mexico. He's got a rap sheet a mile long. Mostly misdemeanors for possession of illegal substances, a few assault charges, and breaking and entering. He's done jail time. Last known address puts him in Tucson. Not sure how he ended up here and he's too far gone to be coherent."

"Take him in," Jones instructed. "Call Dr. Pennington and have him come to the station to do a blood draw and tox screen. I want to know what this guy is on. And where it came from."

"Yes, sir," Ryder said and led Titus back to the cruiser.

The chief turned to Shane. There was a haggard look in the chief's gray eyes. The past few days had taken a toll on the man. "You'll need to come to the station to give your statement, as well."

"Will do, sir," Shane said.

Chief Jones strode away, his gait even but slow. He climbed behind the wheel of his Desert Valley police car and drove away.

Gina walked over. "That was intense."

To say the least. "I'm glad no one was hurt." He steered her to his Jeep. "I have to give my statement at the station. I'm not comfortable dropping you off at the training center."

"I'll go with you," she said as she slid onto the passenger seat.

As he shut her door, he admitted he was glad to have her company and relieved to have her close. With the adrenaline fading, he found himself needing Gina's soothing presence. Something he knew he had no business needing, let alone wanting. He really had to put some distance between them; however, as long as she was his to protect, distance wasn't an option.

Instead, he had to find a way to regulate his response to her. His father would tell him to stop his bellyaching and compartmentalize his feelings. Emotions had no place on the job. Emotions interfered and could result in tragedy.

Way easier said than done. But for Gina's sake, Shane would do whatever was necessary to keep her safe. To keep them both safe.

At the police station, he and Gina entered through the side door just as Ryder was escorting the suspect to the cells.

The man, John, lifted his eyes to stare at Gina. His muddy gaze widened. He lunged toward her. "Are you Maid Marian? Robin Hood is going to rescue you. And me. I'm Little John." He grinned, revealing yellow stained teeth.

Gina shrank back from the man. Shane urged her away.

"What was that about?"

With a sigh, Shane told her about Robin Hood.

"Tim's delusional now," she said. "That makes him more dangerous."

"He's not getting anywhere near you," he assured her.

They stopped at the cubicle that bore his name. He sat at the desk he'd been assigned and wrote up his account of what had transpired inside the convenience store while Gina sat nearby quietly petting Bella. Her presence was distracting. It took him several tries to get the words written in a coherent fashion. So much for compartmentalizing.

When he was finished, he handed the report to Carrie, who'd add it to the case file.

"Ready to go?" Shane asked Gina while resisting the urge to offer her his hand.

"Definitely," she answered as she rose from the chair. "Do you mind if we stop for coffee before picking up the puppies?"

He could use a jolt of caffeine. "Not at all."

"I wish we knew where Marco was," she said as she hitched her purse higher on her shoulder. "Maybe we could check in with the store owners along Main Street and see if anyone has mentioned finding the puppy?"

"If anyone had, I'm sure we'd know. But when we get back to the training center I can make some calls." And just because her brother had escaped from the minimart didn't mean the man wasn't still out there waiting for an opportunity to strike. Shane and Bella had to be on their A game at all times.

A tall, distinguished man in his midforties entered the station, nearly running Gina over. Shane snaked an arm around her waist and drew her out of the way. Which proved a good tactic to keep her from being bowled over, but played havoc with his senses.

"I was summoned by the chief," the newcomer bit out in an impatient tone. He had neatly styled graying dark hair and rimless eyeglasses that distorted his dark eyes. He carried a black bag with the initials W.P.

Taking a guess, Shane held out his hand and said, "Dr. Pennington. I'm Officer Weston. We spoke the other day."

Ignoring his outstretched hand, Pennington said, "Where's the chief?"

"Right here," Jones said as he came out of his office. "Good of you to come, Doctor."

Pennington's lip curled. "Did I have a choice?"

Shane had the distinct impression there was no love lost between the two men. No doubt the animosity was due to their respective relationships with Veronica Earnshaw. Pennington had divorced the woman the chief had considered a daughter.

Granted, Shane didn't know the full story of what had happened between Veronica and the doctor.

"We have a suspect in custody I'd like you to do a tox screen on," the chief said, ignoring Pennington's snide question.

Pennington huffed. "You mean a junkie." He made a face of disgust. "What a drain on society. They clutter up the clinic and keep us from helping those who really need medical care."

"Yes, well." The chief's voice hardened. "The clinic *is* for everyone, is it not, Doctor?"

The two men locked gazes in a battle of wills. Shane exchanged a curious glance with Gina. She gave a slight shrug, clearly unnerved by the power clash in front of them.

Finally, Pennington let out a loud breath. "Show me where you've stashed the criminal."

"This way." The chief led the doctor through a set of double doors leading to the jail cells at the back of the building.

"I sure hope his bedside manner is better when he's with his patients," Gina commented.

Shane touched his hand to the small of her back and led her out of the station. "I can't imagine him and Veronica as a couple. Two abrasive people together…" She shuddered.

"It does seem like a strange pairing," Gina replied. "If I weren't so sure that my brother killed Veronica, I'd wonder if the good doctor didn't have something to do with her murder."

"Spouses and ex-spouses are usually the first suspects in a murder case. But I checked, and the doctor has an alibi."

"Oh, well, then I guess he's innocent. Just not very nice."

After Shane, Bella and Gina were in the Jeep, Shane asked, "How about we grab lunch with our coffee?" His stomach growled.

"That works," Gina said. "I'll call Sophie and see if we can bring her lunch."

"Good idea." Shane headed for the Cactus Café downtown while Gina made the call.

At the café, Gina ordered Sophie a turkey on whole wheat sandwich and a chicken salad on a sourdough roll for herself. Shane ordered a roast beef on rye and a side of fries. They each ordered a coffee to go.

While they waited for their food, they sat on a bench outside the café while sipping from their to-go coffee cups. Bella lay at their feet with a bowl of water provided by the café owner.

Shane surveyed the small community of Desert Valley, feeling a kinship with the people he'd come to know over the past three months. A couple of teenage girls on bicycles rode past. The postman, Charlie, waved from his truck as he drove through town. Bill Baxter swept the sidewalk in front his hardware store, The Tool Corral. A mother and her adult daughter, arms linked and smiles on their faces, entered the Brides and Belles shop.

It seemed like such a peaceful little town. Quaint, even, with colorful storefronts sporting awnings to provide shade from the heat of the Arizona sun. Though today was a mild spring day, he knew in a few short months the weather would turn scorching.

"Do you like living in Desert Valley?" he asked Gina.

"I do." She let out a small sigh. "It's been a nice place to be these past two years. The way the community is so tightly knit. It's a good place to raise a family, too. The schools are good, with high test scores."

He noted her wistful tone and ached for her. He wished there were some way for him to convince her that she shouldn't give up her dream of children out of fear. "You know you could adopt."

She slanted him a quick glance. "True. Or foster. I've toyed with the idea. I think I could provide a stable and loving home for children in need." A small smile touched her lips, drawing his gaze. "I need to stop being a martyr and explore other possibilities. I'll give adoption and/or fostering more serious thought once Tim is no longer a threat to me. Or anyone else."

Pleased to know she hadn't taken too much offense by his blunt comment, he returned her smile. "I think you should. Desert Valley seems perfect."

"Normally, there's not much crime," she said with a grimace. "People tend to look out for each other. At Christmas, the town goes all out with decorations and most everyone attends the community church's pageant." Her voice ticked up in enthusiasm. "There's an Easter parade with kids and adults alike dressed in their Sunday best. Then in May, there's the annual Police Dance and Fund-raiser."

She slanted him a glance, then quickly darted her gaze away. The offer to escort her to the event tripped on his tongue but he wasn't going to set her or himself up for disappointment. Surely by then Tim would be arrested, the cold cases would be resolved one way or another and all the rookies would be on their way to their assignments.

"But I enjoy summer the most," Gina stated firmly. "With the rodeo, the Fourth of July parade and a street fair in August with artisans from all over the state displaying their wares."

He could hear her excitement and love for the town in her voice. It made him ache with longing. He doubted he'd be here to see any of the things she described. And he doubted she'd be willing to leave.

Whoa. Where'd that thought come from? He wasn't about to ask her to uproot her life, leave behind a good job and friends to go with him wherever he was assigned. Once her brother was behind bars, she'd be free to really put down her roots here in Desert Valley, a place she obviously loved.

The café's door swung open and the waitress

stepped out with their bag of food. "Here you are," she said with a smile.

"Thanks, Patty," Gina said as she took the bag.

"Enjoy," Patty said, and ducked back inside.

They walked to the Jeep. With Bella secured once again in the back, they settled in the front seats, and Shane headed toward the training center. He turned onto Desert Valley Road. The screech of tires against pavement was the only warning Shane had before a car shot out from the side street and plowed into them.

# TWELVE

Gina looked out the passenger window and locked eyes with the maniacal stare of her brother behind the wheel of a silver sedan coming straight at her. She barely had time to brace herself before the Jeep was shoved sideways.

The sickening sound of metal colliding, crushing and collapsing reverberated through her, drowning out her screams of terror as she was thrown left then right like a rag doll.

A loud *whoosh* within the Jeep confused her until the dashboard exploded in her face at the same instant the side curtain air bag deployed, slamming into her shoulder. Rough pillows of material nearly smothered her as the Jeep tipped up and then crashed back to earth, landing on all four tires with a jarring bounce.

Her head collided with the side passenger window. The air bag minimized the impact so the window didn't break, but not enough to keep pain from exploding behind her eyes in a shower of bright stars. The world spun. The seat belt dug into her chest and shoulder, pinning her back. Her face flamed and her nose burned from the air-bag residue. Bella's frantic barks punctuated the horror rolling over Gina.

Shane muttered as he worked valiantly to keep the Jeep from rolling. Blindly, she reached for him, but found only air.

Finally, the spinning subsided and the vehicle came to an abrupt stop in the middle of the intersection. Tim's car shot forward and rammed into a light pole.

Eerie quietness stole her breath. Bella! Shane! Were they okay? Her vision danced in and out of focus. Something wet and sticky ran down her face.

Then a hand landed on her shoulder. "You're bleeding."

She swiped a hand over her eyes and forced herself to focus on Shane's face. His green eyes were full of panic as he grabbed his cell and called dispatch. He swiveled to look at Bella. Gina followed his gaze. The dog appeared unharmed. Her ears were standing up, her attention focused on something outside the Jeep. She let out a loud growl followed by a barrage of frenetic barks.

The sudden sound of the passenger-door handle rattling startled Gina. With a yelp, she shrank from the door. A face peered at her. Tim. *Please, Lord, no!*

He bared his teeth and continued to yank on the

door handle, but the metal had been crushed and refused to budge.

Shane kicked open the driver's-side door and rounded the front of the Jeep, drawing his weapon. "Get down on the ground!"

In the back of the Jeep, separated from the front seat by a metal barrier, Bella barked and clawed at the window in a frenzied effort to get to her partner. Shane needed Bella.

Gina tried to pry loose the seat-belt latch, but her hands were too slippery with blood. She wiped her hands on her jeans and reached again for the latch. This time she managed to release the buckle. The seat belt retracted quickly, the metal buckle hitting her in the chin, adding another blast of pain to her already bruised and battered body.

Ignoring the many agonizing places that burned for attention, she scrambled into the driver's seat and out of the Jeep. She hurried to release Bella… but the hatch was stuck. She'd have to figure out another way to free the dog.

She raced to the rear driver's-side door but was momentarily distracted by Shane. He'd holstered his weapon and had her brother down on the ground in the middle of the road. Shane's knee was planted in the center of Tim's back and Shane seemed to be searching his utility belt for something. His handcuffs were missing. Had they dislodged from his utility belt during the crash?

In the fraction of a second it took her to debate

whether to continue her goal of freeing Bella or search for the handcuffs, Tim burst into action. He reared up with a loud roar and bucked Shane off. Shane stumbled back and landed on his rear while Tim shoved to his feet and ran. Before Shane could regain his feet, Tim had reached the crowd of bystanders that had been drawn to the accident.

The shrill cry of sirens filled the air. Too late. Her brother was escaping. They needed Bella. Gina pivoted, intent on crawling in the Jeep.

*"Gina!"*

Tim's shout froze her in place. She met her brother's crazed stare. Even from this distance, malice gleamed like a flame in his eyes. Her heart thudded in her chest. Her brother, her twin, hated her. Her mind couldn't grasp the concept. His mental illness may be driving him but at some point he had to take responsibility for his actions. They were connected by blood, yet were so far apart in every other way that he was a stranger to her.

A stranger with a desire to kill.

And she was his target.

She staggered back a step. A piercing wail sounded in her head. Pain exploded in her chest, making each breath difficult. She pressed a hand over her heart.

Two police cars arrived and skidded to a halt. The sudden silence released Gina from her panic. Chief Jones and Officer Bucks exited the chief's vehicle while James Harrison and Ellen Foxcroft climbed out of another with their canine partners.

Tim turned and raced toward the woods and quickly disappeared into the shadows of the trees and brush. Shane jumped to his feet with his weapon out, but there were too many people between him and Tim.

Shane quickly explained to the chief and officers what had happened.

James's lip curled. "We'll get him this time." He tugged on the leash attached to his bloodhound, Hawk. "Let's go, boy."

The two headed for the woods with Officer Bucks following closely behind. Gina sent up a quick prayer of safety for the trio.

Shane glanced toward the Jeep. Meeting his gaze, Gina rushed to yank open the Jeep's rear passenger door. Anchoring herself with her back against the driver's seat, she grabbed the metal tension grate, tugging on it with all of her strength. Finally it gave and she was able to push it aside to allow Bella to jump out. The dog raced to Shane's side and Gina followed, stopping next to him.

He holstered his weapon and then gripped her by the shoulders. "Are you hurt?"

She laid her hands flat against his chest. His heart hammered beneath her palms. She searched his face, wincing at the dark bruise forming on his cheek. "No. Thankfully. You?"

"A bruised ego." A muscle ticked in his strong jaw. "I can't believe I let him escape."

"You stopped him from getting to me. That's all that matters." Staring into his handsome face she was inundated with relief that they were both alive and unharmed. The strong urge to kiss him slammed into her. Her breath caught and held. Did she dare? It would be reckless and foolhardy, but the need was nearly overwhelming. Instead, she dropped her head forward to hide her flaming cheeks. "I owe you my life."

Shane's arms slipped around her and drew her close. She clung to him, grateful to God above that they both were alive.

Ellen hurried to Gina's side with gauze pads and pressed them to her forehead. "An ambulance is on its way."

When it arrived, the chief insisted Gina and Shane go to the hospital to be checked out by a doctor.

Gina wasn't thrilled to ride in the back of the ambulance, but when Shane and Bella jumped in, she had no complaints. They sat side by side on the bench usually reserved for the paramedic, with Bella at their feet. He slid an arm around Gina again, pulling her close. She laid her head on his shoulder, concentrating on the feel of his solid grip holding her tightly as a way to keep the aftermath of the trauma from turning her into a sobbing mess.

When they arrived at the hospital, the orderly led

them to the emergency room. Shane grasped her hand as they walked. The pressure of their palms pressed together soothed her more than any medicine could. Though she had to admit her head throbbed and her body ached from being thrown around during the crash.

"Officer Weston, we'll take you over here." A stout nurse gestured to an open curtained room.

"No." The protest was out before Gina could stop it. She didn't want to be separated from him. He was her anchor. She was afraid that without him by her side she'd succumb to the hysteria that had built up inside of her during the ordeal.

Shane squeezed her hand. "It'll be all right. Bella will stay with you."

"This way, Miss Perry," another nurse urged.

Reluctantly, Gina let go of Shane's hand to follow the nurse. Bella's nails clicked on the tiled floor as she kept pace with Gina. *Breathe*, she told herself. *Just breathe. You're safe now. Tim can't get to you here.*

The nurse handed her a gown. "Put this on. The doctor should be with you soon. Do you need help?"

She clutched the gown to her chest. "No, I can manage."

When the nurse left, Gina finally succumbed to the horror. She staggered to the exam table and leaned against it as the full impact of what they'd just survived hit her like a rogue wave. Her chest grew tight. Her breathing constricted. Her mind replayed what had happened. Tim had crashed a car into the side of Shane's Jeep in an attempt to kill her. He wanted her dead. There was no mistaking his intent.

But he hadn't succeeded.

Would he ever stop trying?

Bella nudged her in the thigh as if sensing her dark thoughts. Grateful for Bella's presence, Gina squatted to hug the dog, a liberty she only dared take with the police dog because she had trained her. It was kind of Shane to let his partner come with her; he obviously understood that Bella would ease Gina's fears. His compassion touched her deeply. He was a good and honorable man. A man she was swiftly falling for. How crazy was that?

After hurriedly donning the gown, Gina waited for the doctor.

Shane. He'd become such an important part of her life in such a short amount of time. She knew the trauma and tension of the past few days had had an effect on her judgment, but she couldn't discount the very real attraction and affection she harbored for the handsome rookie.

If things were different, if she were different, she could see herself giving Shane her heart. As it was, she struggled to keep her emotions in check. The last thing she needed was to become attached to Shane. Not only was he leaving, but she couldn't ever saddle anyone with the danger of her DNA.

Tonight had brought home once again that faulty genes and bad decisions ran in her family.

With a sinking sense of doom and a heart that felt as if it were cracking open wide, she reminded herself that Shane deserved better than that. "You were fortunate, Officer Weston. You and Miss Perry both," claimed the doctor, who'd introduced himself as Dr. Ruskin. He was older, with a shock of white hair and pale blue eyes that seemed to see right through Shane.

Shane didn't believe in luck. God had put a hedge of protection around him and Gina, preventing Tim from doing more damage beyond totaling the Jeep. They'd been blessed, that was for sure. If only Shane hadn't let Tim take advantage of Shane's momentary distraction when he'd realized his cuffs were missing. Inexcusable.

His father would be mortified. And he could just hear the jabs his brothers would aim at him. *Loser. Weakling. Mama's boy.*

Shane shoved away the echo of his brother's taunts and concentrated on the doctor. "Can I go now?"

He needed to see Gina, to assure himself that she hadn't suffered any major injuries.

"Yes," the doctor replied in a tone that had Shane waiting for more. "I'd advise you both to rest for the next twenty-four hours at least. The bruises you sustained to your ribs need to heal before you are too active. And the same goes for Miss Perry. Though she's a bit more banged up than you are."

Shane winced with concern. He'd seen the laceration on her forehead from the air bag deploying. He wasn't sure what other injuries she'd sustained during the crash.

He changed back into his uniform and went in search of Gina and Bella. Every moment away from them ratcheted up his tension.

He found them waiting at the administration desk. The stark white bandage wrapped around Gina's head glared in contrast to the tumble of red waves cascading over her shoulders. Her hazel eyes were clear, but her smile appeared strained. She looked tired and scared and pretty all at the same time.

The rush of relief at seeing her caught him by surprise. As he moved toward her, he tried to analyze what he was feeling. But his emotions were in a jumbled mess, so dissecting his feelings wasn't happening.

She closed the distance between them and he automatically opened his arms for her to step into his embrace. It felt like the most natural act in the world. Holding her close, tucked within the shelter of his arms—that was where he wanted her. Always. A pipe dream, but for now, he wouldn't fight his emotions. After the ordeal they'd been through, he just didn't have any fight left.

"Hey, you two," James Harrison said as he sauntered through the hospital double doors and halted beside them. Hawk, his bloodhound, greeted Bella. The police dogs all had a special place in their hearts for their former trainer. "Thought you might need a ride home."

"We do," Shane said. "Did you track down Tim Perry?"

James's jaw tightened. "I'm sorry, I didn't. The guy's slippery. He had another vehicle stashed not far away. The one he used to ram into your Jeep was stolen from a house down the block."

"He must have followed us from the Cactus Café," Gina said.

"Yes, and anticipated we'd be crossing that intersection on the way back to the training center." Shane hated to admit it, but Tim was smart. An evil genius. But one of these days he'd make a mistake that would land him in jail for good. At least Shane prayed so.

James drove them back to the training center. As soon as they entered, Sophie hugged Gina. "I freaked out when I heard what happened. Are you okay, for real?"

"I'm a little banged up, that's all." Gina hugged her friend back. "The seat belt did a number on my ribs." She touched the bandage around her head. "Not to mention the stitches on my forehead and in my scalp where I hit the window."

Shane hadn't realized she'd banged her head, as well. He was surprised she didn't have a massive headache. Must be the pain meds that would eventually wear off. He wanted her home before then.

"Thank God above you two are safe and relatively sound," Sophie stated.

"I'm sorry to leave you with all the work here," Gina said.

"Nonsense," Sophie replied. "For now I can handle the center. Until we can open back up for training sessions, there isn't much for me to do. Though I have had two breeders call to say they have dogs old enough for training. I told them we aren't offering sessions but that I'd take the pups and start working with them to get them ready for when we do offer police training sessions again. And I've also put out a call to departments all over the state for refresher courses. When you're ready to come back there will be plenty of work but until then rest and recover from the crash."

Shane noted the way Gina grimaced. He touched her arm. "See, nothing to worry about here."

Gina sighed. "I know. I just feel responsible for everything that has happened. So many people's lives have been affected."

"You're not to blame," Shane told her, but he could tell by the look in her pretty eyes she still held herself accountable for her brother's evil acts.

"He's right," Sophie said. "Don't beat yourself up for your brother's actions. When he's caught, life will get back to normal and we'll open back up for training."

Which would mean Shane would be gone, assigned to another department, either in Flagstaff or somewhere else in the state of Arizona. Somewhere far from Desert Valley. The thought left a bitter taste in his mouth.

"In the meantime," Sophie continued, "I've organized the supply closets, gone over the accounts and scrubbed every square inch of the place." She frowned. "Except for Veronica's apartment upstairs. I can't bring myself to go in."

"I don't blame you," Gina said with a visible shiver. "I'll be back tomorrow to help you if you'd like."

He admired her willingness to be there for her coworker, but she needed to look out for her own well-being. "The doctor said you need to rest for at least twenty-four hours," he reminded Gina.

Shane scooped up the puppies and escorted Gina out. James dropped Shane, Gina and the puppies off at the condo while he and Hawk went back to the station.

"I'll take care of these two while you rest," Shane told her as he set the puppies on the floor. They immediately ran for the back patio door.

"There's no way I can sleep right now," she countered. "Can we watch a movie?"

Her question socked in him in the gut. An image of the two of them snuggling on the couch like a couple in love marched through his mind. His pulse picked up. As tantalizing as that thought was, they weren't in love. They weren't a couple. They were just two people who'd endured a harrowing event and needed some downtime to decompress. He could handle that. "Sure, but first I'm going to put these two out back and then make us something to eat."

Ten minutes later, with the puppies chewing on bones and Bella lying on her bed, Shane and Gina settled on the couch. A lunch of cold cuts and cheese, bread slices and two apple ciders was laid out on the coffee table. Gina picked a movie from the On Demand function on the cable box as she nibbled at the food. Shane wanted to urge her to eat more, but refrained. The last thing she needed was him bossing her around. Before long, she abandoned the food to curl up next to him.

His chest grew tight. The image he'd had earlier was coming true. He should move away from her, stop this madness right now, but it felt too good having her so close. And as he settled his arm around her, he knew there was no way he'd break this moment for anything.

She rested her head on the soft plane between his chest and shoulder, fitting perfectly within his embrace. Warmth spread through him and he couldn't help but feel protective of this sweet woman. He knew there were other emotions floating through his system—affection, caring, attraction. As much as he wanted to deny that he was growing attached to this beautiful woman, he couldn't.

It was going to be torture to leave her behind when he left. But he would leave and she would stay. That was the way of their jobs.

And he needed his focus on his career, not on a woman, if he hoped to earn his father's and brothers' respect.

Though that driving need that had propelled him through his life didn't have the same intensity it once had. Being here in Desert Valley, away from the influence of his family, he found himself questioning his needs. Questioning his path in life.

As Gina's breathing evened out, he glanced down to find her sleeping in his arms. For a long time, he held her, savoring the feel of her against him. When the movie ended and he had no legitimate reason to keep holding her, he lifted her and carried her to her room. Bella followed.

Awkwardly juggling Gina, he pulled back the blankets and then laid her down. He slipped off her shoes, then settled the covers over her. Bella rested on the floor at the foot of the bed. The puppies trotted in and headed for their crates. Afraid the two young dogs would wake Gina, Shane dragged them and their beds into the hall. They'd sleep in his room tonight.

Shane paused at Gina's bedroom door and gave the hand command for Bella to come with him. She stood and came to him but then turned to look back at the woman on the bed. Bella sat and nudged him in the thigh.

Was she trying to tell him she wanted to stay with Gina?

Seemed his partner was as smitten as he was.

Leaving the dog there added another measure of safety. He crouched down so he was at eye level with Bella. "Okay. You stay here and protect Gina," he whispered.

Bella immediately moved back to the end of the bed to lie down. She settled her chin on her paws and closed her eyes.

Marveling at Bella's intellect, he left the door slightly ajar in case Gina awoke and needed him.

His heart spasmed as the thought seared clean through him. He wanted her to need him. No one had ever needed him. But Gina did and that made him feel invincible. And foolish.

How was he going to say goodbye when the time came?

Gina awoke to find Bella standing beside her bed. The dog cocked her head and then walked to the door, which was cracked open. Bella glanced back at her, clearly wanting out, but also wanting her to follow.

Blinking the sleep from her eyes, Gina realized she was fully clothed. She must have fallen asleep on the couch with Shane and he'd put her to bed. And he'd left Bella with her as protection.

Tenderness filled her. Shane's thoughtfulness set her heart beating. He was such a caring man.

Honorable and committed. The type of man every woman hoped to find.

That they'd been thrown together by danger only added to his appeal, because he could have refused the assignment of guarding her. He could have been cold and distant in dealing with her but he wasn't.

He was personable, concerned for her comfort and safety. She knew he would protect her at all costs. He'd taken an oath to protect and serve. And yet she hoped his actions stemmed from more than just duty. Could he care for her beyond an assignment? Did she want him to?

And did she care for him?

Of course she did. He'd put his life on the line for her. But what she felt went beyond gratefulness and that scared her because she knew there could be no future for them. Her shoulders slumped. She had to protect Shane as much as he was protecting her. She needed to keep things between them from turning personal. They could be friends but nothing more.

She slipped from the bed, every muscle protesting, and opened the door all the way. Bella waited for her and walked at her side into the living room. Shane was in the kitchen with his back to her. His broad shoulders filled out his dark blue T-shirt nicely. The puppies came running, tumbling over themselves to get to her. She knelt to receive their love. Bella headed for the back patio door. Shane hustled over to open it for his partner.

"How are you this morning?" Shane asked, his green-eyed gaze searching her face.

"I feel like I was in a car accident," she replied as she gingerly sat on a stool at the counter. The puppies lost interest in her and chewed on their toys.

He gave her a lopsided grin that made her breath catch. "Yeah. Me, too."

Forcing herself to breathe evenly, she said, "Thank you for last night."

Heat flooded her cheeks as she remembered how she'd snuggled up next to him on the couch. She'd been so worn-out and emotionally drained she hadn't had the mental fortitude to stop herself. "I mean for leaving Bella to watch over me through the night."

"You're welcome."

Best to put last night behind them. "So I guess today we stay here."

He nodded. "Doctor's orders."

She smiled, thinking there were worse ways to spend a day than with a handsome man, two puppies and a guard dog on duty. Just as long as there was no more snuggling. Or kissing. Even if she yearned for more.

She knew this forced proximity was necessary, and she'd enjoy it while it lasted. But she'd have to put a lock on her emotions if she hoped to make it through this situation unscathed. The wounds to her flesh were nothing compared to the potential wound to her heart.

# THIRTEEN

Though they'd been housebound for the day, Gina decided the best use of their time, and the best way to keep things between her and Shane on a more professional level, was to continue working with the puppies while reviewing Shane and Bella's training.

There'd been some hysterical moments where they'd both ended up doubled over with laughter at the antics of the puppies. Bella had even proved a good teacher for the two rambunctious pups by using her herding instincts to keep Lucy and Ricky in line.

All in all a good day. And after dinner, when it was so tempting to curl up on the couch with another movie and a potential opportunity to snuggle with Shane, Gina opted for reading in her room. She told herself that wasn't disappointment she'd glimpsed in Shane's eyes when she'd wished him good-night.

When she'd awoken this morning, she'd found Bella sleeping in the hall outside her bedroom door, which had melted her heart and made her seek out Shane to thank him.

"Hey, I'd like to take credit," Shane said with a smile. "Once you went to bed last night, she took a position in front of your door and wouldn't budge."

That made her feel so loved. At least by the dog. She ignored the tiny, mopey voice inside of her that wished Shane loved her.

Time to get back to work.

James dropped Gina, Shane and Bella off at the training center on his way to the station with Hawk. He and the other rookies would continue helping in the investigation into the two previous rookies' mysterious deaths and the cold case of Melanie Hayes's murder.

If Shane was disappointed not to be more involved in the investigations because he had to protect her, he didn't say so. Gina felt bad regardless. If her brother hadn't come to Desert Valley with murder on his mind, then the rookies would now be far away at various police departments around the state, and Marian Foxcroft wouldn't have had to so generously endow the police station with the funds to keep the rookies on staff.

Strange how life had a way of changing so dramatically, so quickly. Her father would have said God takes the bad in life and uses it for good. She wasn't so sure that was true, but at least now Ryder could solve his wife's murder, and the questions that surrounded the two other mysterious deaths might be answered. She prayed so.

Her cell phone rang as they entered the training center. Shane set the puppies free while she grabbed her phone from her purse. Her ribs ached with every movement but she forced herself to ignore the pain. The doctor had said only time would heal the sprain in her rib cage from the seat belt locking so tight across her torso. She'd taken off the bandage covering the few stitches on her head, opting to let the wound breathe now that it had stopped bleeding.

She stared at the caller ID and didn't recognize the number. Fear tightened her throat. Would Tim call? She met Shane's gaze. "I don't know who this is."

"Put it on speaker."

She did as he instructed. "Hello?"

"Is this Gina Perry?" A woman's crisp voice spoke through the speaker.

"Yes, this is Gina."

"Marian Foxcroft here. I understand you've been caring for the two puppies, Ricky and Lucy."

Relaxing, she nodded. Then quickly answered, "Yes, ma'am."

"I take it there's been no word on where little Marco is?"

Gina's stomach clenched. "No, there hasn't. We've put up flyers, we've gone door to door as well as searched the area surrounding the training center."

"I will offer a reward for the puppy's safe return. Surely that will galvanize the person who took him to come forward."

"That's very generous of you." Gina couldn't stop the spurt of excitement. If someone had found Marco maybe they would want the money more than the puppy. She sent up a quick prayer that puppy would be found alive. That he hadn't become food for a predator.

"I'd like to see the other puppies," Marian said, interrupting Gina's prayer.

"Of course. I'm with them now at the training center. We'd love for you to visit us."

"No. I want you to bring them to me. I'm sure their mama would be happy to see them."

Gina raised her eyebrows. Though the puppies had stayed with their mama long enough for the mother dog to remember them, Gina doubted the dog longed for her puppies. Dogs didn't have the same emotional attachment to their offspring as humans do, even if this litter was the mama dog's first.

More likely Marian Foxcroft was lonely up in that big house of hers. Though Gina knew Ellen lived at home, the young rookie wasn't often there, preferring to work rather than deal with her mother. Empathy for the older woman had Gina agreeing.

"Yes, of course I can bring the puppies to you. We could be there in an hour."

"Thank you, Gina. I appreciate that." Marian hung up.

"Why did you say you'd take the puppies there?" Shane asked with a frown. "We need to keep a low profile. Stay here or the condo. After yesterday, I don't want you out and about."

As much as she wanted to agree with him that staying in safe places was the smart thing to do, she didn't want to be a prisoner to her brother's madness. "We can borrow the training center's SUV. I'm sure Sophie won't mind. Besides, Marian Foxcroft isn't someone we can say no to. She funds the center as well as your salary."

He blew out a breath. "Fine. But I'll let Ryder know where we're going in case we run into your brother again."

Gina's tummy twisted at the thought, but she refused to live her life in fear. They would take the necessary precautions. Besides, God was on their side.

Between the two, she, Shane and the puppies should be all right. Shouldn't they?

The Foxcroft home sat on a five-acre rise east of Desert Valley in an exclusive and secluded neighborhood. It was rumored some of the houses in the area belonged to celebrities. Gina wasn't sure she believed the rumor, since she'd never seen anyone she recognized from television or the big screen around town. But whoever owned the sprawling homes out here definitely had money, just like Marian Foxcroft.

On the way in, with Shane driving, they'd passed some big spreads, but the Foxcroft house was by far the most impressive to Gina. After entering the code Marian had texted them earlier, they passed through an ornate wrought-iron gate and drove up the long drive.

Though maybe not as big as some of the other mansions they'd passed, Marian's butter-yellow multilevel Victorian-style house sat back from the road like a regal queen. Dormer windows and a curved veranda with large bay windows added character. Smaller multipaned windows graced every wall, no doubt providing a panoramic view of Desert Valley and the scenic landscape in all directions.

Gina smoothed the front of her slacks as she climbed out of the training center's SUV, suddenly wishing she'd changed into something more presentable than her work clothes. It wasn't every day she was invited to visit Marian Foxcroft.

She harnessed and leashed the two puppies before they could dash off to explore unfettered. She let the dogs have a quick break before tugging on the leash to corral them in as she and Shane headed up the walkway.

At the foot of the cedar stairs that led to an ornately carved, knotty pine front door, his cell phone rang. She paused with a foot on the stair as he stopped to check the caller ID.

"It's the chief," he said. "You go on in, I'll be right there."

She nodded and urged the puppies up the steps. On the wide porch, the puppies sniffed the edges of the colorful flowers and greenery growing in the numerous clay pots.

From inside the house a dog's deep bark could be heard. The mama dog sensing intruders? Or greeting her puppies?

Gina rapped her knuckles against the solid wood door. The force of her knock pushed the door open. It hadn't been closed all the way. The fine hairs on her arm rose and a shiver tripped down her spine.

Caution tightened her shoulders as she strained to listen. The only noise she heard was the now frantic barks of an adult dog.

After a heartbeat, she called out, "Mrs. Foxcroft? It's me, Gina Perry. I have the puppies with me."

No answer. Gina glanced back at Shane. He had his back to her as he talked with the chief. For a moment indecision warred within her. Did she go in and investigate or wait for Shane? But how long would he be?

The puppies leaped up the short doorstep, pushed the door wide and took off, practically dragging Gina behind them. She dug in her heels in an effort to stop them, but that even as their trainer, she'd only been working with them a few short days and was no match for their combined weight and power.

Hurrying to keep up, Gina followed the puppies across a gleaming cherrywood-floored foyer to a vaulted ceiling great room at the back of the house. In the corner was an extralarge kennel housing a beautiful adult German shepherd. The puppies' mama.

But it was the woman lying prone on the plush white area rug that forced the breath from Gina's lungs.

Marian Foxcroft.

Gina's legs buckled. She went to her knees. *Not again. Oh, please, God.*

A dark, crimson stain marred the light-colored fibers beneath Marian's head. Her eyes were closed, her complexion nearly matching the carpet.

"Shane!" Reeling in the puppies so that they didn't contaminate the scene, Gina crawled to Marian's side. With a tight grip on Ricky and Lucy's leash in one hand, Gina pressed the shaky fingers of her free hand against the pulse point on the older woman's neck and braced herself for another tragic death.

But Marian had a pulse. Weak, but definitely there. Gina's shoulders collapsed with relief. Marian was unconscious but alive.

"Shane!" Gina yelled again, putting all her strength into her voice.

Who would do this? She fumbled to grasp her

cell phone from the bottom of her waist pack as the question rattled around her brain. Why would anyone want to hurt Marian? Gina couldn't see her brother doing this. Why would he?

As she yanked her cell out, a baggie of treats dropped to the ground. The puppies lurched for it, each taking a corner.

Gina dialed 911 and then wedged the phone between her ear and shoulder while she wrestled to get the baggie from the pups. The last thing she needed was the bag to tear open and dogs treats to go flying all over to contaminate the scene, making it harder for Shane to do his job. She pulled the dogs farther away from Marian.

When the dispatcher answered, words gushed from Gina. "We need an ambulance at the Foxcroft house." She spit out the address from memory. "Hurry, please. Marian's bleeding from a head wound."

The dispatcher assured Gina the paramedics were en route.

"Hang in there, Marian," Gina whispered to the center's benefactor. "Help is on the way."

The pounding of feet on the hardwood floor announced Shane had heard her cry. Marian's German shepherd burst into another volley of barks at the newcomer as Shane burst through the archway into the living room with his weapon drawn. His gaze landed on her then bounced to Marian.

Surprise crossed his face before a shuttered look overtook his features.

Slowly, he holstered his gun and stepped closer. "What happened?"

Not liking the wariness in his tone, Gina grew defensive. "She was like this when I came in."

A muscle in his jaw jumped. He moved to check her pulse.

"Alive," she was quick to assure him. "Barely. I've called 911. An ambulance is on its way."

"Good." His gaze swept the room. "Don't move or touch anything. I'm going to clear the house."

He pivoted with his hand on his weapon and stalked out from the room. He couldn't really believe she'd done this, could he?

A sense of déjà vu hit her hard. Shane's first reaction when he'd come upon her and Veronica had been to suspect Gina of murder. But they were long past that now, weren't they? What would she have to gain from hurting Marian?

Nothing. And if Shane didn't know her well enough by now to know she wouldn't do this...

But hadn't she been telling him she had her brother's blood in her veins? That she and Tim shared the same genes? That somewhere in her DNA malice lurked, waiting to be released? So why wouldn't his reaction be suspicion?

She slumped. That it hurt was her problem. A problem she had to get a handle on fast.

She may be many things, but a masochist wasn't

one of them. From this point on she would guard her heart with every ounce of energy she possessed.

Letting herself care about Shane, about his opinion of her, was detrimental to her well-being. If she hoped to resume her normal life once her brother was captured, she had to remain detached, unemotional.

She could feel a hardening taking place and she prayed God would understand. Somewhere in the recesses of her mind, she remembered reading once that the quickest way to distance oneself from God was to have a hard heart.

But to protect herself from the pain of a broken heart that was exactly what she needed to do.


Shane moved from room to room, checking closets and under beds. No sign of an intruder except for the rear patio door. It stood wide open. Bingo.

He stepped out onto the back patio. There was no sign of the intruder. The large dog run to the left was empty. And no one lurked on the lush lawn, which extended to the edge of the property and opened to a long stretch of desert before converging with the outer rim of the forest that dominated one side of the valley.

Marian's attacker was long gone.

Was it Gina's brother?

No, that didn't make sense. Why would Tim Perry want to hurt Marian Foxcroft? How would he even know about her?

Something else was going on here. What it was, Shane didn't have a clue.

He retraced his steps back to Gina's side. She glanced at him, her hazel eyes clouded with anxiety. He could only imagine how horrible this was for her.

After everything she'd been through these past five days and then to add more trauma to the mix by finding Mrs. Foxcroft rendered unconscious by obvious foul play, it amazed Shane that Gina wasn't hysterical. He certainly wouldn't blame her for having a meltdown. She was due.

Anger churned in his gut. He'd come so close to capturing her brother and ending this ordeal for Gina. And it chafed his ego and pride that he'd allowed Tim the opportunity to escape. Shane had been distracted when he'd realized his handcuffs were gone. If only the handcuffs hadn't dislodged from his utility belt during the crash, Tim would be in custody and Gina would be safe and…Shane frowned as he realized Gina would still have found Marian unconscious and bleeding.

If Shane truly believed Tim wasn't the culprit here, then who was?

He touched Gina's shoulder. "The ambulance should be here any moment."

She moved away and picked up her phone from where it lay on the ground. "I should call Ellen."

"I can do it," he offered, wanting to make this easier for her.

"That's okay." She scrolled through her contact list. Her hands shook so badly that Shane thought she might drop the phone.

He covered her hands with his own. "Let me do this."

She relinquished her hold on the phone and scrambled away. "Okay." The sound of sirens had her rising to her feet. "I'll meet the ambulance. And put these two in the SUV."

As he watched her hurry out of the room, taking the puppies with her, he had the strangest feeling she was trying to get away from him as much as she was anxious to bring help to Marian.

He pressed the number under Ellen Foxcroft's name. She answered on the second ring.

"Gina?"

"Actually this is Shane. Gina's with me. We're at your house." He sought the right words to say. "We found your mother unconscious when we arrived."

"I heard. I'm almost there," the other K-9 rookie stated, the tension in her voice tugging at Shane. Despite the rocky relationship between mother and daughter, Shane had no doubt Ellen loved her mother.

He hung up as the paramedics hurried in with Gina close behind. Shane moved out of the EMTs' way and stepped to Gina's side. They watched in silence as the medics tended to Marian's wound and put her on a stretcher.

A few moments later Ellen Foxcroft rushed in as

the paramedics wheeled Marian toward the front door. Ellen clasped a hand over her mouth. Gina hastened to put an arm around Ellen.

"Who would do this?" Ellen asked. She reached out to touch her mother's hand.

Gina shook her head. "I don't know. There was no one else here when we arrived. She'd called me and asked if I'd bring the puppies out for a visit."

Ellen visibly got ahold of herself. "We have to find the person who did this."

"Can you tell if anything is missing? Maybe this was a robbery gone bad," Shane suggested gently.

"What else could it be?" Ellen's voice rang with anger. She walked to the fireplace in the corner and pointed to an empty spot on the mantel. "There's a statue missing. A silver poodle that was a gift to my mother from the mayor."

The German shepherd in the crate whined at Ellen. She put a hand on the kennel door. "Gina, would you mind taking Amber to the training center? I'll come get her later."

"Of course I will," Gina quickly answered.

"Ma'am, we need to get your mother to the hospital," one paramedic said. "Do you want to ride with us?"

"Yes, thank you." Ellen left with the paramedics, passing Chief Jones and Officers Bucks and Harmon as they entered.

Shane explained the situation to the newcomers. The chief tilted his head and addressed Gina.

"When you approached the door, there was no sign of a break-in?"

"None, sir," she said. "The door was unlatched. I called out for Mrs. Foxcroft but there was no answer. I stepped in and found her there."

"I cleared the house and found the back patio door open, as well, but there was no sign of tampering with the locks on either the front or the back door," Shane supplied.

Officer Bucks elbowed Harmon and said in a low voice, "Isn't this the second body she's discovered? A little too coincidental, don't you think?"

Gina gave a little gasp at the accusation.

Shane whipped his attention to Bucks. "Hey, don't go disparaging Gina. She didn't hurt Mrs. Foxcroft or kill Veronica."

Bucks held up his hand. "Whoa, there, boy. Didn't mean to rile you up over your girlfriend."

Anger and dislike spread hot through Shane, and he ground his teeth together as he stepped toward Bucks. The craving to plow his fist in the older man's face was strong.

"Enough." The chief's voice brought Shane to a halt. "Bucks, Harmon, I want this place dusted for prints now."

"Yes, sir." Harmon held up a black box by the handle. "I anticipated the need."

"Brownie points for you." Bucks sneered. "Come on, let's get the front door first."

Shane blew out a calming breath and met Gina's wide-eyed gaze. Red stained her cheeks. He hated that she had to hear Bucks's inflammatory remarks and that she'd witnessed Shane nearly losing it. He wasn't usually so easily provoked, but the snide way Bucks talked about Gina had set something primeval off inside of Shane.

Chief Jones shook his head. "I'm not sure what I'm going to do with those two." He shrugged. "Sorry about that, Gina."

"I didn't do this," she said. "I didn't hurt Marian."

"Of course you didn't," Shane said, upset that she'd even have to defend herself. "And anyone who could think such a thing doesn't know you."

Her lower lip trembled. Confusion swirled in her hazel eyes. "Thank you, Shane."

Afraid she'd break down and cry in front of their boss, Shane gestured to the mantel, hoping to direct the conversation back to the assault. "Ellen said a silver statue is missing. Most likely the weapon used on Marian."

The chief rubbed his chin. "If it wasn't a break-in, then Marian knew her attacker. And if the statue was used, then perhaps Marian had invited the person into the living room. They argued and the perpetrator reached for the nearest heavy object and bashed Marian over the head."

"And left her for dead," Shane pointed out. "If

we hadn't happened to have an appointment with Mrs. Foxcroft it could have been many hours before Ellen came home and found her."

"Do we think this could be the work of Tim Perry?"

The chief's question echoed Shane's earlier thoughts. "Sir, I don't think so. First, I can't imagine Mrs. Foxcroft inviting him in, and second, there's no reason for him to go after her. It's his sister he wants to harm."

"Right." The chief heaved a beleaguered sigh. "The assault on Marian is a separate deal. We need to dig into what Marian has been doing lately that would motivate an attack like this."

Officers Bucks and Harmon reappeared in the archway of the living room.

"Both doors have been wiped clean," Officer Harmon announced.

"All right, people," the chief said. "Let's clear out. I'm calling the Flagstaff crime lab to come in and do a full forensic search of the house and grounds. Hopefully there's a clue waiting to be discovered. I hate the thought of two maniacs running loose in Desert Valley."

Shane couldn't have agreed more. Suddenly the previous deaths that Marian Foxcroft had asked the rookies to look into took on a more ominous meaning. Had Marian's attacker been lurking in town for the past five years? Had the request to solve the cold cases been the motivation for the assault on Marian? And what lengths would the person go to in order to keep the past mysteries unresolved?

# FOURTEEN

At the police station, Gina and Shane were separated as part of standard procedure in an investigation where there was more than one witness. Each was sent to a room to write out their account of finding Marian unconscious in her home.

Alone in an interrogation room, Gina tried to recount every detail she could remember about the visit to the Foxcroft home. Her hand shook so hard, her writing looked like that of a kindergartener.

The horror of finding Marian lying unconscious and bleeding twisted Gina up inside. She couldn't grasp why someone would hurt the older woman. She was so generous to the town, to the police department and the training center. Though not the most personable woman in town, Marian's roots were deep in the community.

Poor Ellen. She had to be beside herself with worry.

Gina understood the heartache of losing a parent. She knew the agony of watching her father die at her brother's hand. That night would forever be etched in her mind. The terror of seeing her brother grab their father's service weapon from his holster, seeing the shock on Dad's face as he realized what Tim was doing.

Dad had tried to talk Tim down. He'd reasoned, cajoled and demanded, but Tim's manic state only worsened. He'd felt threatened and claimed Dad was trying to keep him from his full potential. But Dad had only wanted to help his son.

And Tim had killed him for it.

With a shudder, Gina pushed the memories to the recesses of her mind and finished the report. She stepped out of the room and headed toward the chief's office. No one was there.

She wandered farther down the hall to the conference room. Through the interior window she could see a meeting in progress. All of the rookies and the Desert Valley police officers were sitting or standing around an oblong conference table listening intently to what the chief was telling them from his place at the head. She hesitated, not wanting to disturb them.

"Are you done?"

Startled, Gina whirled around to find Carrie Dunleavy, the police department secretary, standing behind her. "Oh, Carrie. How are you?"

"Good, thank you." Her gaze went to the papers in Gina's hand.

"Yes, I'm done. What should I do with this?"

Carrie held out her hand. "I'll take it and add it to the file."

"Thank you." Gina handed over the report.

Carrie patted her arm. "Just so you know, I don't believe you hurt Marian, despite what anyone else thinks."

A knot formed in the pit of Gina's stomach. It seemed Officer Bucks had made his opinion well-known very quickly. "Uh, thanks."

Carrie walked away, her shoes clicking on the linoleum.

Gina remained in the hallway, unsure what to do next. She peeked into the conference room again in hopes of catching Shane's eye, but he was focused on the heated conversation taking place. If Carrie were to be believed, Gina was the topic of discussion.

Just then Whitney Godwin glanced toward the window, meeting Gina's gaze. The sympathy in the rookie officer's expression curdled the breakfast in Gina's stomach. Needing to get away from the station and the sense of accusation permeating the air, Gina headed for the side exit. She drew up short.

The door had a warning sign that it was an alarmed exit and to please use the main entrance to come and go from the building.

She spun around, intending to go back to the front of the building, but who was she kidding? She couldn't leave. Not without Shane.

Her brother was still out there somewhere.

She felt trapped and condemned. She veered from the exit and entered the women's restroom. After slipping off her waist pack and setting it on the wooden bench, she splashed water on her face.

Tears leaked from her eyes to mingle with the water running down her cheeks. How could anyone believe she had attacked Marian Foxcroft?

Shane didn't. He'd defended her when Bucks made his outrageous claim that she was responsible for Marian's injury.

And he hadn't corrected the officer when he'd stated she was Shane's girlfriend. Because the accusation was so ridiculous that Shane hadn't felt the need to set Bucks straight? Or because there was some part of Shane that wanted her to be his girlfriend? Wishful thinking on her part.

She gripped the side of the sink and willed herself to stop crying. She wasn't weak. She wasn't crazy and she wasn't capable of hurting someone else. She wiped at her eyes and stared at her reflection in the mirror.

She may share Tim's DNA but she wasn't like him. She was like her mother.

And her fear was just that—fear. She'd allowed fear to rule her life for too long.

Not anymore. Shane had shown her how to be brave.

Shane believed in her. More than she believed in herself. He made her want to allow love into her life. He made her want to be strong. Strong enough to know that she was done hiding here in Desert Valley.

Yes, her brother wanted to kill her. She wasn't a martyr and she wasn't suicidal. But once he was caught and jailed, then she would leave Desert Valley. She'd start over somewhere else. She'd done it once. She could do it again.

With Shane?

Sorrow twisted in her chest. No, not with Shane. He was committed to staying in Desert Valley until the mysterious deaths of the two rookies and Melanie Hayes's cold case murder were resolved. And now with Marian Foxcroft having been assaulted, all the men and women of the Desert Valley police force were needed.

She could wait for him. Then they could leave together.

However, she had no idea if he felt the same.

The same?

How did she feel about Shane?

She'd come to rely on him. She trusted him in a way she'd never trusted anyone else. She respected him and cared for him.

Was there more?

Her heart thumped against her ribs. Yes, she felt more than she'd been willing to admit. She'd fallen for him. With her whole heart. She loved him.

She leaned her forehead against the cool surface of the mirror. Now what was she supposed to do?

Survive long enough to be able to leave Desert Valley.

With or without Shane.

Despite the ache in her heart.

"There's no proof Gina Perry isn't guilty of attacking Mrs. Foxcroft. She had motive and opportunity," Officer Bucks stated with a smirk on his thin lips. His pale blue eyes sparked with animosity.

"Come on, really? She didn't have motive." Fisting his hands, Shane couldn't keep his exasperation from showing. Bella leaned into his leg. The dog had to sense his upset.

Shane had written out his report detailing the events at the Foxcroft place before joining the others in the conference room. He swept a look over the rookies and the established officers seated at the large table or standing against the wall of windows running along both sides of the conference room, giving the space a fishbowl feel.

Shane and the other rookies had each been issued a dark blue Desert Valley police uniform that matched the other officers'. Until now Shane hadn't really felt like part of the police force, even though he wasn't wearing this uniform. His assignment of protecting Gina had kept him isolated from the collective.

He was relieved to see the incredulous expression letting him know they weren't buying Bucks's outrageous claims either. Shane sent an imploring look to the chief, seated at the head of the table. "Chief, you can't believe what Bucks is spouting? Gina did not hurt Mrs. Foxcroft." Shane shot Officer Ken Bucks a seething glance.

"She went in alone and had time to crack Mrs. Foxcroft over the head before you went in," Bucks volleyed back with distain. "Maybe she and her brother are in this together. Like some twisted version of Bonnie and Clyde."

It was all Shane could do not to throttle the older officer. How on earth could the man think she and Tim were in cahoots? The man had a screw or two loose. "Are you nuts? Tim Perry is trying to kill her."

Shaking his head with frustration and anger, Shane didn't understand why Bucks was pushing so hard to throw Gina under the bus. "Gina had no reason to hurt Mrs. Foxcroft."

"Maybe Mrs. Foxcroft asked to have the puppies back?" Bucks said, folding his arms over his chest. "Gina seems pretty attached to the mutts."

"Of course she's attached." Whitney Godwin spoke up, her voice hard-edged. Her canine partner, a tan-and-white Pointer named Hunter, lifted his head to stare at her. "She's the puppies' trainer. That's her job."

"Maybe she was hoping with Veronica gone, she'd be lead trainer," Bucks said.

"That's ridiculous." Shane fought to keep from shouting. "And certainly not motive to hurt Mrs.

Foxcroft. We already have a suspect in mind for Veronica's murder—Tim Perry."

"Has the statue been found?" Ryder asked quietly, drawing the room's focus. He sat at the far end of the table opposite the chief. Titus, his yellow Lab partner, lay panting on the floor. A bowl of water was beside him.

Officer Eddie Harmon shifted in his seat to face Ryder. "No. Marlton and I searched the house and the property. There was no sign of any silver poodle statue or any fingerprints beyond Mrs. Foxcroft and her daughter, Ellen."

"Whoever assaulted Mrs. Foxcroft took the statue with them," James said. "Hawk followed a scent to the edge of the property line where there were tire tracks."

Shane threw his housemate a grateful glance.

"Same tread as the tracks found after Tim Perry crashed the stolen sedan into Shane's Jeep?" Tristan McKeller asked, referring to the place where Hawk had lost Tim's scent. Jesse, Tristan's canine, lay under the table at Tristan's feet. At the sound of his partner's voice, his tail thumped against the floor.

James shook his head. "No, these were different."

"We'll know who attacked Marian when she awakes." The chief pinned a dark look on Bucks. "Ken, no more disparaging talk of Gina. She's not a suspect." He rubbed a hand over his weary face. "Where are we on the investigation into Veronica's murder?"

Ryder laid his hand on a file folder in front of him. "The ballistics report on the bullets used in Veronica's murder came back."

Shane's gut clenched in dreadful anticipation.

"They matched the striations on the weapon found at the train depot."

Confirming Shane's grandfather's SIG-Sauer P220 was indeed the weapon used to kill Veronica.

Air left Shane's lungs in a rush. His chest tightened. He reached for his inhaler inside the pocket of his pants but didn't bring it out as he willed his breathing to even out. So not the news he'd wanted to hear. He still didn't know how someone had gained his fingerprint, enabling them to open his safe and take the weapon. Whoever had killed Veronica had done so with willful intent.

But what did this do to the theory that Tim Perry was Veronica's murderer?

"Wait a minute," Tristan said, straightening in his chair. At his feet his partner stirred, obviously sensing Tristan's tension. "Are we still going with the assumption that Tim Perry killed Veronica when he couldn't find Gina at the training center?"

All eyes turned to the chief. But it was Ryder who answered, "I'm inclined to say Veronica's killer wasn't Tim Perry."

A stunned silence met his calm and grim pronouncement.

"We won't know for sure until we capture Tim Perry and question him," the chief said.

Shane wasn't so sure it would be that cut-and-dried. He had a very bad feeling that things were not as they seemed.

"Was Shane's handgun used in any other crimes?" Bucks asked Ryder. "Like your wife's murder."

Shane clenched his jaw tight. The man had no tact. "No. There's no way my grandfather's handgun was used in another crime. My grandfather was still alive and in possession of the weapon five years ago."

"Shane is correct," Ryder stated. "Veronica's murder is the only crime on the handgun."

"And where are you on Melanie's murder?" The chief's tone, though not gentle, was at least respectful, unlike Bucks's.

"Sifting back through evidence," Ryder stated.

Shane couldn't imagine how hard that had to be.

Chief Jones gave a short nod then turned his attention to the others. "The Riverton and Miller cases?"

"The same, sir," Tristan answered. "Combing through the reports and evidence files of both cases."

Though Whitney didn't verbally respond, she nodded an affirmative to Tristan's statement.

"Okay, good. Let me know if you come across anything that might have been missed or could be further explored," the chief said. "Weston and Harrison, I want your focus to be on the Perry situation."

"Yes, sir," Shane and James said in unison.

"Then we'll adjourn." The chief stood and walked from the room.

Bella rose to all fours, her head tilted to the side. Her ears perked up in alert mode.

Unease slithered down Shane's spine. The last time she'd exhibited this same behavior had been the night they'd found Gina with Veronica's dead body. He put his hand on Bella's neck. "What is it, girl?"

Hawk also scrambled to his feet and lifted his nose to the air. He let out a guttural growl that turned into a howl.

Shane had a bad feeling. He needed to find Gina.

A scrape of noise behind the closed door of the stall next to the exterior wall made the hairs at Gina's nape rise in alarm. She'd thought she was the only one in the restroom.

The two-foot by two-foot sash bathroom window was open. Unease threaded through her, making her break out in a cold sweat. Had that been open when she entered the restroom? She couldn't remember.

She glanced under the stall doors but saw no feet indicating there was another person in the restroom with her.

*This is a police station. You're being silly.* With a rueful shake of her head, she turned back to the mirror. Hadn't she just decided she wasn't going to let fear rule her life? And yet she was jumping at the slightest provocation.

The last stall door on the end burst open and her brother charged out.

She yelped with a burst of terror and lunged for the door, but Tim grabbed a handful of her hair and yanked her backward. His sweaty palm clamped over her mouth, stifling the scream that finally broke loose.

"Shut up!" He whispered the harsh command into her ear. "I'll kill you here and now if you make any noise."

Her mind scrambled to make sense of the situation. He'd climbed through the window, just as he had at the training center. No one had anticipated he'd try to get to her inside the police station. It boggled her mind that he'd be so bold. Had he been waiting inside the stall? How could he have known she'd enter the bathroom? Had he been watching her? But how?

"Do you understand me?" He tightened his hold on her hair, ripping strands from her head.

She nodded as tears of pain and panic crawled up her throat and burned her eyes.

"Good." He met her gaze in the mirror. Eyes the same shade of hazel as hers stared at her, but the malice in Tim's gaze sent terror zinging through her like a pinball.

Twigs and dirt clung to Tim's dark auburn hair. He smelled of body odor and damp earth. His crossbow clung to his back, the fletching of arrows sticking out of a pouch attached to the bow. His clammy hand made her skin crawl as he slowly lowered it from her mouth to wrap his fingers around her throat. "We're going out the window."

Not in this lifetime.

He was going to kill her anyway, right?

Better to die knowing she'd put up a fight. Maybe someone would hear and come to her rescue, because if she let him take her from here, the next time anyone saw her would be when they stumbled upon her remains out in the desert.

Fierce anger filled her. She was ready to do what needed to be done to stop him.

He dragged her to the window and shoved her hard. "Climb out."

She braced her hands on either side of the window, her fingers clutching the window jambs. She planted her feet where the wall and floor met. "No."

Tim drove his shoulder into her back in an effort to force her out the window. Pain in her kidneys nearly took her out but she breathed through the pain and let loose a loud scream that reverberated off the tiled walls.

Fisting her hair in his hand once again, he dug the tips of his fingers into the soft flesh of her throat, pressing against her esophagus, cutting off her scream and choking her. "Fine. We'll go out the side door. And just to be clear, after I kill you, I'll go after every cop I see. I'll take down as many as I can before they get me. Those deaths will be on you."

She swallowed the bile burning a hole through her, and she sent up a silent plea to God above. *Help me stop him, Lord. Please.*

Keeping his hand gripped in the soft tissue at her throat, he opened the bathroom door with his other hand to peer into the hall. It was empty. He opened the door and pushed her through. The exit was steps away.

Hopeful anticipation rumbled through her.

Once he pressed the metal bar running across the center and the door opened, the alarm would sound.

He'd bring the police running on his own. She'd have to make sure he couldn't use his bow to hurt anyone.

But would she be strong enough?

Shane's heart beat in his throat as Bella led him past the empty interrogation room where he'd last seen Gina. Where could she have gone?

Bella sniffed the floor. Shane prayed she picked up Gina's scent. Bella moved away from the interrogation room and headed down another hallway that led them past the backside of the conference room.

The sudden, jarring sound of the alarm system jolted Shane's heart into high gear. Bella barked and strained at her leash. Letting out the lead, he raced after her as she ran, the tapping of her nails drowned out by the siren. She led him down a short corridor that ended with an emergency exit. The door was slowly closing.

"Gina!" Shane shouted. He couldn't hear anything over the alarm.

Shane and Bella rushed for the door. Hitting it with his shoulder, Shane burst out of the police station and into the side parking lot. Bella put her nose to the ground. Making a zigzag line, she crossed the lot to an empty space where a car had been. His heart dropped. Gina was gone.

# FIFTEEN

A band of panic pulled taut across Shane's chest as he surveyed the empty parking spot where a car had once been. Bella had led to this spot. Where was Gina? What had happened to her?

He didn't believe for a second she'd left of her own accord. Her brother had somehow infiltrated the police station and kidnapped her. Or killed her and taken her body away.

The thought made him stagger back a step. *Oh, Lord, please no.*

No, he couldn't let his mind go there. She had to be alive. There had to be a chance of saving her.

Shane had promised Gina he'd keep her safe. He'd failed.

Bella whined as she paced in a circle, clearly as upset at losing Gina as Shane. They'd both fallen for the lovely trainer. Shane's breath hitched. He'd fallen in love with Gina. The ramifications of the realization rippled through him. But now was not the time for examination or analyzing. Gina's life was in danger.

"Shane!" Whitney Godwin called from the side exit to the police station. "We found something."

Something? Not Gina. Please not Gina. He and Bella hustled back inside and followed Whitney to the women's restroom. He crowded inside. James and Ryder were there. The window in the exterior wall was open. On the bench beside the sink lay Gina's training pouch.

His stomach sank. She wouldn't have willingly left this behind. Pulling on gloves, he lifted the pouch and checked inside, confirming what he feared. Her cell phone lay nestled among the treat bags.

Tracking her through her phone wasn't going to happen.

"Everyone back to the conference room," Ryder said. "We need to come up with a plan to find Gina and Tim Perry."

"Her one hope is if the canines can trail her scent." Though Gina's scent would be on her pack, it would be muddled by the dog treats and whoever else had handled the pack. Shane grabbed James by the arm. "I'm going back to the condo to get Gina's pillowcase. Her scent will be the strongest on that."

"Agreed." James handed over the keys to his truck and then glanced toward the conference room door. "I'll cover for you."

Grateful to his fellow rookie, Shane accepted the

keys, and he and Bella hurried out of the station house. At the condo, Shane rushed to Gina's room and stripped her pillowcase off the pillow. He held the material to Bella's nose. "Gina. We have to find her, Bella. Gina. Find Gina."

They jumped back into the truck. When they returned to the police station James and Hawk were waiting. Shane released Bella then handed James the pillowcase. James offered its scent to Hawk. The dog let out a woof.

Bella gave an answering bark.

Ryder and Titus stepped outside, followed by Whitney and Hunter, and Tristan and Jesse. The pillowcase was handed off to each handler to let his or her K-9 partner have a good whiff of the special scent that was Gina.

Chief Jones and the other officers filed out, as well.

The chief pinned Shane with a tense look. "The next few hours are critical. We'll fan out and start searching."

Shane nodded. If Tim Perry was as bent on killing Gina as he seemed, he'd do the horrendous deed within the first couple of hours. And then he'd be in the wind.

Rage like he'd never experienced before engulfed Shane. When he found Tim Perry, Shane intended to make the man pay for all the terror he'd caused his sister.

"Ken and Harmon, you ride with Tristan and

Jesse. Start at the train station and run the tracks.
Whitney and Hunter, you'll ride with me. We'll
head back to the training center and work from
there. Marlton, you go with Ryder and Titus. Start
your search in town and move south," the chief instructed. "James and Shane, you and your partners
work together from here." He encompassed them
all with a sweeping glance. "Watch each other's
backs."

The officers of the Desert Valley Police Department headed off to start their search for Gina Perry.

As Shane gave Bella another whiff of Gina's pillowcase, he prayed they were on a rescue mission
and not a recovery one.

The old beater station wagon chugged along,
bouncing over every rut and pothole on the fire
road cutting through Desert Woods. After Tim had
forced Gina into the back of the wagon, he'd tied
her hands behind her back and toppled her over,
demanding she stay down or he'd run anyone she
tried to contact over.

She'd stayed lying sidewise on the bench backseat for as along as she could, but once they'd gone
off the road, she'd worked her way to a sitting position. Without the use of her hands, though, she
was unable to brace herself as the wagon took another jolting hit. Her teeth snapped together with
the impact. The wagon groaned. The thing was on

its last legs. She expected the transmission to drop out any second.

In front of her, Tim sat in the driver's seat, clutching the steering wheel and staring out the dirty front window with singular concentration.

"Tim, talk to me," she said for the umpteenth time. "I don't understand what you want. What do you hope to accomplish?"

He continued to ignore her. She wiggled closer to the door and tried as subtly as she could to grasp the handle, but it was just high enough to be out of her reach. Frustration washed over her and she barely refrained from kicking the back of Tim's seat.

That he hadn't killed her outright was a blessing, but she had no doubt he had some nefarious plan for her demise. The farther they drove away from town, the more worried she was that Shane and Bella wouldn't be able to find her. She didn't even have her cell phone, so they couldn't use that to locate her. Despair crept into her consciousness but terror remained prominent.

She licked her dry lips, thankful the windows were open to offer some relief from the stench of the vehicle, though the dust swirling through the interior clogged her throat and nose, making her cough.

Looking out the window, she tried to gauge where they were, but since she hadn't taken the time to explore Desert Woods, she wasn't sure how far away the Desert Pines campground was or if they were anywhere near it. Maybe they were closer to Valley Lake at the other end of the woods, or near the water, which was an arm of the Colorado River. The area was massive and the landscape alternately treacherous and beautiful. How was Shane going to locate her?

She was going to have to find a way to escape and get help for herself. If she could alert someone, then they could call for help. But so far they hadn't passed anyone after leaving the town.

Tim made a sharp left turn. Gina slammed up against the door, her shoulder taking the worst of the hit. "Hey!"

The way became even more jarring as they bounced off the fire road and blazed a trail through the woods, barely missing a tree. He finally slipped the station wagon behind a large tangle of bushes and cut the engine.

A cloud of dirt enveloped her through the open windows. Her body was racked with a coughing fit as she tried to expel the dust from her lungs.

Tim got out and walked away.

Gina twisted in the seat, trying to keep him in her sight. What was he up to?

He disappeared around the tangle of bushes. She studied the dense foliage and realized the bushes weren't a naturally occurring bramble. Tim had forged out a fort of bushes, tree limbs and rocks.

So this was where he'd been hiding the past few days. How long had he been here?

With him out of sight, she tried again with less subtlety and more awkward groaning since her hands were tied behind her back to get the door unlocked and opened. Finally the lock released and the door popped open. She practically fell out of the wagon. She rolled the rest of the way out, tucking in her chin and landing on her back, smashing her hands beneath her.

She sat up and wiggled to get her feet beneath her. Afraid Tim would return, she searched for the way they'd come in but couldn't discern the path they'd taken. Didn't matter. She needed to move. To escape. Better lost in the woods than meekly awaiting her fate at Tim's hand.

She darted behind a tree and glanced up through the branches and leaves. Maybe she could navigate her way back to town using the sun to set a course. If she kept the ball of fire at her back, then she'd be heading west. Or was it east? Or did she need to move toward the sun, which would mean she'd be traveling south? She wished she'd paid better attention to her astronomy class in college. She just had to pick a direction and pray it was the right one.

She pushed off from the tree and sprinted away.

"Oh, no, you don't!" Tim screeched from somewhere behind her.

She didn't dare look back. Keeping her focus on the way in front of her, she hopped over an exposed root, only to land on her foot wrong. She went down. Without her hands to break the fall, her head hit the dirt with a thud. She scrambled back up despite the pain exploding behind her eyes. She had to keep moving.

A hand grabbed her arm and hauled her off her feet. Tim threw her down on the ground. She screamed and kicked at him but he danced out of her way. He huffed as he towered over her. "I'm not done with you yet."

He yanked her to her feet. She let out a yelp at the sudden pain in her shoulder. He dragged her stumbling back to his fort and shoved her inside the makeshift shelter. She fell heavily onto her knees but the pain barely registered. Tim came in behind her and plopped down on a cot.

The space had the cot, a small cooking stove and pint-size generator for electricity. A light had been strung up and a laptop computer sat on the dirt floor. A pile of filthy clothes was stacked in the corner. How could he live like this?

Her gaze met his. The malice she'd seen before was gone. He looked tired, regretful. He'd come down from his mania. Maybe there was still hope he'd let her go.

In a gentle tone that she'd heard their mother use with him, she said, "Tim, why are you here?"

"For you."

"How did you find me?"

His lips spread into a grim smile. He pointed to the computer. "No one can hide from the mighty internet."

She struggled to comprehend what he meant. She didn't have any social-media outlets and was careful not to let herself be photographed.

"There was a publicity shot of the center. You were in the background," he said. "I knew you couldn't stay away from dog places. I combed the Internet looking for you. I'd know you anywhere."

Her heart sank. Veronica had set up the publicity event. Gina knew the shot he referred to, but Gina had had her back to the camera. She'd been so sure no one would be able to recognize her. But Tim had. And the photograph had brought him to the center. Where he'd hoped to find her but instead had found Veronica. "Why did you kill my boss?"

Tim tucked in his chin. "I didn't kill her. I locked her in the closet. If she died while in there that's not my fault."

"What?" Oh, he meant Sophie. "No, I mean when you first came to the center last Saturday night. I wasn't there but you found my boss, Veronica. The lady that was in the photo you saw. You killed her when you couldn't find me."

He shook his head, his gaze confused. "No, I didn't. I did go to the center that afternoon and saw you there. But you left before it got dark and went home then to the church where you were serving food." He giggled. "You spilled gravy on the floor and that guy slipped. That was funny. I decided to wait for you at your house. I didn't kill anyone."

His words slammed into her. She had spilled some soup and Carson Lloyd, a banker in town, had slipped. She'd been aghast. He'd asked her out and she'd declined.

"I wasn't going to grab you at the church, though." Tim wrinkled his nose. "I don't want to bring down the wrath of God on me."

Gina's mind tried to make sense of what he was telling her. He'd followed Gina to church and then went to Gina's home to wait for her to return. He hadn't killed Veronica.

Then who did kill Veronica?

The same person who assaulted Marian Foxcroft?

Mysteries Gina hoped she lived to see resolved.

Right now she had to find a way out of here. "Tim, I have to go to the bathroom. Can you untie me? Let me go, please?"

"There's a can in the corner," he said.

She clenched her jaw to keep her temper under control. "Why are you doing this?"

"You're my sister. We need to be together."

"You've been trying to kill me the past few days!"

"Yeah, sorry about that." He stood. "Want something to eat? I caught a squirrel. They aren't too bad."

She gagged at the thought. "No, I'm not hungry.

Tim, please let me leave. I won't tell anyone where you are. Just let me live my life in peace."

"No!"

"You need help," she said. "Don't you see that?"

His face hardened and that malicious gleam returned. He moved swiftly to stand in front of her and poked her in the chest with his finger. "Don't you dare be like Dad or you'll end up dead like him." He grabbed her by the arm and forced her up and into a camping chair. He tied her feet to the legs. "Now, shut up. I'm tired."

He lay on the cot and rolled onto his side, away from her. After a few minutes, his snoring filled the shelter.

Unbelievable. If she weren't so terrified, freaked-out and scared, she'd laugh with hysteria. Instead, she set to work on trying to free her ankles from the leg of the camping chair. She sent up a prayer that help was on the way and it arrived before her brother changed his mind and killed her.

# SIXTEEN

Shane jogged behind Bella, with James and Hawk just off to his right side. The dogs had found a scent in the air and they were trailing it through Desert Woods. Shane had already had the campground ranger check all the cabins and campsites, but he'd come up empty. Had Tim somehow slipped past the ranger?

Bella and Hawk were leading them not to the campground but to the fire road, which gave the forestry service access to the lake and the river whenever there was a fire in the region. There were tire tracks in the dry earth. Shane couldn't tell if they were recent or not.

Bella lifted her nose to the air and swerved to the left. Hawk kept moving forward then doubled back and hurried after the other dog. Shane shared a curious glance with James as they veered left to follow the dogs.

All the dust and dirt of the forest floor made Shane itch and tightened his lungs. He fingered his inhaler, yet he was unwilling to stop to use it. The panic he'd been keeping at bay edged closer, crowding out his focus. But he had to stay on task and detached so he could be an effective officer.

Losing it wouldn't do Gina any good.

Both dogs stopped and sat in front of a large tangled mess of bushes and branches. Not a natural structure. Heart beating in his ears, Shane drew to a halt. He gestured for James to go left around the crude shelter while he and Bella would go to the right. There had to be an opening. Would he find Gina inside? Alive or dead?

Pain craved a hole in his heart. He sent up a prayer that God would see them through this.

Bella sniffed the air and the ground as they rounded the rudimentary lodging. An old-style station wagon, battered and dirty, was parked on the back side of the snarled mass of debris. Bella alerted in front of a makeshift door fashioned from branches and chunks of moss. Anxiety twisted him up inside.

James joined him with Hawk. Shane withdrew his sidearm; James followed suit. Shane counted down with his fingers. On three they breached the manmade lodging.

"Halt, police!" Shane shouted as he rushed inside. He took in the scene, quickly cataloging that Gina was half out of a chair with one ankle tied to a leg. She blinked up at him in stunned surprise.

Tim scrambled up from the cot with a large knife

in his hand. Tim's gaze darted between Shane and Gina. Shane understood the other man's intent just as he lunged for Gina.

"Don't!" Shane shouted. Bella barked. Hawk howled. James aimed his weapon at Tim's head.

Tim ignored the order and wrapped one hand around Gina's arm, yanking her close. The knife hovered over her throat. "Back off!"

Not willing to risk hitting Gina with a bullet, Shane used the best weapon available. "Attack!" Shane gave Bella the command.

The dog didn't need any more encouragement. She leaped at Tim, her teeth sinking into his hand that held the knife. Bella's paws landed on the chair beside Gina's head. Tim screamed, the knife dropped to the side to land on the ground, and he released his hold on Gina. She scrambled away from her brother as best she could with her hands tied behind her back. James moved in and subdued Tim.

Shane holstered his weapon to gather Gina in his arms. He quickly untied her hands and her ankle. His pulse thundered in his veins; his heart pounded. "I feared I wouldn't get to you in time."

Relief washed over him as he captured her lips before she could say anything and kissed her with all the pent-up anguish, longing and love he could pour out.

James cleared his throat, snapping Shane back from the brink of losing himself in Gina.

"You want to call Bella off?" James asked with a wry twist of his lips.

The dog still had Tim's hand in her teeth.

"Release." Immediately she did. Then she jumped down and came to Gina and licked her face. Gina hugged Bella.

"I'll just take him out and call the chief," James said with a grin. Then he pushed Tim out of the shelter. Hawk followed them.

Gina gazed up at Shane with eyes bright and full of tears. "I was so scared but I knew in my heart you two would find me."

"I've never been this frightened before," he admitted. He cupped her cheek. "I don't know what I would have done if I'd lost you."

She turned her head to place a kiss in his palm. "Thank you." After a moment, she looked to him. "Can you help me to my feet?"

He jumped up and lifted her off the ground, then slowly set her on her feet. He pulled her close for a hug and kiss, thanking God that she was safe. A few minutes later they walked out of the shelter hand in hand.

They were crowded into the conference room. Shane stood behind Gina's chair, his hands warm on her shoulders. She couldn't stop herself from reaching up to place her hand over his. That he'd found her in the middle of the woods was a feat she'd despaired wasn't possible. Her relief at seeing

Shane and Bella had been overwhelming. Seeing Bella in action had been amazing. Though she'd trained many dogs over the years to take down a suspect, she'd never seen a dog in action during a real crime. Now her respect for the K-9 officers and their partners had tripled. Her job was important, and the officers and their canines were critical in the field.

And now with her brother in custody, the adrenaline and fear seeped from her, leaving her feeling weepy and joyful and exhausted all at the same time.

But what had her heart still thumping in her chest was the way Shane had tended to her. He'd been gentle, loving. His kiss lingered on her lips, making them tingle. They hadn't had a moment alone since they'd walked out of Tim's makeshift shelter, so she hadn't told Shane how she felt. She wasn't sure she was brave enough to.

"Thank you, Shane and James," the chief said in a voice choked with pride. "You will be receiving commendations for your service in bringing in the prime suspect in Veronica's murder."

"Uh, sir," Gina spoke up. "Tim didn't murder Veronica."

All eyes swung to her. The room filled with stunned silence.

Shane's hands flexed against her collarbone. "What are you saying?"

She looked up at him. "I asked him why he killed her but he said he didn't."

"Of course he'd deny it," Officer Bucks spat out. "He's a criminal. He's not going to confess to murder so easily."

She shook her head and turned her gaze to Chief Jones. "Sir, I believe Tim. He found me from the publicity shot that Veronica had had taken for the center. He came to the center and followed me home and then to the church, where he spied on me before he returned to my house to wait for me. He was trashing my house at the time of Veronica's death. Veronica's murderer is still out there."

Everyone started talking at once. The chaotic noise filled Gina's head, making her temples throb.

"Excuse me," Carrie Dunleavy called from the doorway.

The chief held up a hand, calling for quiet. "Yes, Carrie?"

"Chief Weston of the Flagstaff PD is in your office. He'd like to speak to you and Officer Weston."

Gina's gaze jumped to Shane. What was his father doing here? His jaw tightened and his green eyes glittered with concern. Her heart squeezed tight. She prayed the elder Weston wasn't here with bad news.

He leaned down to whisper in her ear. "I have to go talk to my dad. I'll be back."

She nodded as he removed his hands from her

shoulders, leaving cool spots that sent a shiver racing through her.

"Okay, folks," the chief said. "We've jobs to do. Ryder, you take point on questioning the suspect."

Jones tipped his chin toward Shane. "Officer Weston, after you."

The two men left the room with Bella at Shane's side. Gina remained seated while the others filed out of the conference room. Carrie Dunleavy moved to stand next to Gina.

Gina glanced up at Carrie with a questioning look. "Is everything okay?"

"I just wanted to say I'm glad you're okay," the station's secretary said. "We were all worried about you."

"Thank you," Gina replied, touched by Carrie's sentiment. Gina decided she needed to make more of an effort to befriend the woman.

"Too bad Weston will be transferring out sooner than expected," Carrie said. "I was under the impression you two had a thing going on."

Gina swallowed back the surprise bubbling up inside of her. So that was why his father was here, to insist that Shane be released to join the Flagstaff PD. Her shoulders slumped with disappointment because she knew that was Shane's goal—to work with his family. She didn't even have the fortitude at the moment to correct Carrie's assumption that there was more going on between Gina and Shane than there actually was.

"Carrie, I hear the phone ringing," Whitney Godwin said as she plopped down in the chair next to Gina, her canine, Hunter, at her feet.

"Oh, thank you." Carrie turned and hurried away.

Whitney touched Gina's arm. "I can't imagine how hard this has been for you."

"It's been an ordeal," Gina confirmed. "Tim needs help. I hope now he'll get it."

"And what about you and Shane?" Whitney wagged her eyebrows. "Is Carrie right? Do you and the handsome rookie have a thing going on?"

Needing to confide in someone, Gina faced her friend. "I've fallen in love with him."

Whitney's eyes widened and a smile spread across her pretty face. "I thought so. You two are so good together. I could tell you both had feelings for each other during the training."

"Well, it doesn't matter, because he will be leaving," she replied. "Whether it's now or later."

"Then go with him," Whitney said in a tone that suggested the thought was a no-brainer.

"I don't know if he feels the same."

"You haven't told him how you feel?"

Gina shook her head. "No."

"You should. Don't wait. Take it from me, if you delay in confessing your feelings, you might miss the opportunity and then…" Whitney trailed off, her gaze taking on a faraway look, and sadness dampened her expression.

"Whitney?" Gina wondered if her words were more personal than just advice. Whitney had never named the father of her baby.

"Just tell him before it's too late," Whitney said.

"Is that what happened to you?" Gina tugged on her bottom lip, debating whether to mention the conclusion she'd come to when she and Shane were babysitting Shelby. "Whitney, is Brian Miller Shelby's father?"

Startled, Whitney stared at Gina. "How did you…?"

"Shelby has Brian's green eyes." She touched Whitney's hand. "When you and Brian were in the training session last year I had a feeling you and he were seeing each other."

"You never said anything."

"I didn't want to pry." Empathy cramped her chest. "It must have been hard for you to have a baby alone. I wish you'd have confided in me. I would have helped you."

A tear welled in Whitney's eye. "I wish I had. I was going to tell Brian that night, but then the fire happened and it was too late." She wiped at her tears. "I didn't get a chance to tell my brother either before he was killed in Afghanistan."

Gina hugged her. "Oh, honey, I'm so sorry. I'm here for you—you know that, right?"

Drawing back, Whitney nodded. "Thank you. I appreciate that. I've felt so alone. But I have my neighbor and her family. They take good care of Shelby when I'm at work."

"That's good, but don't close yourself off to love. One day you'll meet someone who will fill the void left by Brian and your brother."

Whitney arched an eyebrow. "I could give you the same advice."

With a rueful smile, Gina agreed. "Yes. I should take my own advice."

Whitney sobered. "So if your brother didn't kill Veronica, then who did?"

Shifting back to the question of the day, Gina couldn't stop the shudder coursing over her. "I would hazard a guess it was the same person who hurt Marian Foxcroft."

"Probably. She's in a coma, you know."

Sympathy twisted Gina's insides. "I was sorry to hear that. I'll pray she wakes up soon."

"Me, too." Whitney leaned closer and lowered her voice. "I've been looking into Brian's death. For all intents and purposes it does appear like an accident. But I knew Brian. His family died in a house fire. There is no way he'd have ever lit that candle, let alone put it in a place where it would topple over and catch the house on fire."

A chill skated across Gina's flesh. "As much as I hate to say this, I think we have a serial murderer in our midst."

\* \* \*

"Dad, stop," Shane said, holding up a hand to cut off his father's diatribe. They stood in the chief's office facing each other. Dad was dressed in his chief's uniform, all his medals and bars reminders of his status. "You don't get to make this decision."

Dad wanted Shane to be released from his obligations here in Desert Valley and return with him to Flagstaff. But Shane wasn't going to bow to his father's expectations or rants. He'd done enough of that in his life. "I've agreed to stay on here until the department's unsolved cases are resolved."

"You did your part by bringing in that criminal," Trent Weston said between clenched teeth. He was a man who expected others to bend to his will.

"I did, but there's more work to be done." Shane glanced at the chief, who sat behind his desk taking in the family drama playing out before him. Shane didn't blame Jones for not wanting to intervene. Family dynamics could be tricky. Shane refocused on his dad. Though he was at his father's eye level, Trent Weston had an intimidating presence that made him a formidable chief of police and father.

"Look, Dad, when it's time for me to leave Desert Valley, I'll be going wherever I'm assigned, whether that's Flagstaff or some other department in the state."

"That's not what we agreed to when you left for your training."

"True, but I've decided that I need to live my

life for me. Not you." Gina had made him realize how much he'd been living to please his family rather than to fulfill his own destiny that God had planned for him.

Dad pressed his lips together and narrowed his gaze. "If you change your mind, you know where to find me."

With that his dad spun on his heel and stormed out. Shane stared after him. Wow, that had gone way better than he'd anticipated.

"Good for you, son," the chief said as he rose. "Now, we've got work to do. If Gina is to be believed and her brother didn't kill Veronica, then we have a murderer still loose."

"I do believe Gina, sir," Shane said.

"Then let's get busy." The chief led the way out of his office.

Shane went in search of Gina and found her still in the conference room with Whitney. When he stepped into the room, Whitney jumped up from the chair. "I'm sure I've got to be somewhere." She sent Gina a look rife with unspoken meaning. "Don't wait."

Whitney grinned at Shane and then she and Hunter left the room.

"What was that about?" he asked as he took the seat next to Gina.

She swallowed as she faced him. Her eyes were huge in her face. Something was wrong. Concern arched through him. He gathered her hands. "What wrong?"

Her fingers laced through his. "Nothing is wrong. I have something I need to say."

Why did that sound so ominous? "Okay."

"You may not want to hear this, but I need to say it before I lose my nerve," she said, her voice trembling. "I know you're going to leave Desert Valley. Probably sooner than later, but I can't let you go without telling you that I, uh, well—" She took a deep breath. "I love you, Shane Weston."

If he hadn't been sitting, her words would have knocked him flat on his behind. She loved him. Joy like he'd never experienced blasted through him, making his chest tight and his breathing restricted, but no inhaler was needed. "I feel the same way," he managed to say past the lump in his throat.

"What?"

He breathed in and let it out slowly as a calm happiness took hold of him. "I love you, Gina Perry. I think I have since that first day I walked into your training class."

A delighted smile spread over her lovely face. "Really?"

"Yes, really." He leaned in and planted his lips against hers. They kissed for several minutes of pure bliss. When they broke apart, he said, "I don't know what the future holds or where I'll end up assigned to, but would you... Do you think you'd, uh, well, be willing to..." He couldn't believe how badly he was botching this up. How did he ask her to leave her life for him?

"Yes," she said.

He stilled, daring not to hope she meant what he hoped she meant. "Yes, what?"

She grinned. Her hazel eyes sparkled. "Yes, I'll go wherever you're assigned."

He let out a relieved sigh. "I'm so glad to hear that."

Then he kissed her again.

\* \* \* \* \*

*If you liked this* ROOKIE K-9 UNIT *novel,*
*watch for the next book in the series,*
TRUTH AND CONSEQUENCES
*by Lenora Worth.*

Dear Reader,

I hope you have enjoyed the first installment in the Rookie K-9 Unit continuity series from Love Inspired Suspense. Writing about the men and women who work with police K-9 dogs has given me a great appreciation for the work of the K-9 officer and handler team. As a dog lover I enjoy incorporating canines into my stories.

Gina was able to work with many men and women and a variety of dog breeds as a trainer. Pairing her with Officer Shane Weston was a good match, just as Shane and Bella were a good match. Both Shane and Gina had personal issues to deal with that made falling in love difficult, but eventually they were able to let go of the past and find it in their hearts to let love in.

I know you'll enjoy the upcoming books in this series, as the authors are all fabulous, and it has been a privilege to work with them.

May God bless you abundantly,

# LARGER-PRINT BOOKS!

## GET 2 FREE
## LARGER-PRINT NOVELS
## PLUS 2 FREE
## MYSTERY GIFTS

*Love Inspired®*

# SUSPENSE

RIVETING INSPIRATIONAL ROMANCE

## Larger-print novels are now available...

**YES!** Please send me 2 FREE LARGER-PRINT Love Inspired® Suspense novels and my 2 FREE mystery gifts (gifts are worth about $10). After receiving them, if I don't wish to receive any more books, I can return the shipping statement marked "cancel." If I don't cancel, I will receive 4 brand-new novels every month and be billed just $5.49 per book in the U.S. or $5.99 per book in Canada. That's a savings of at least 19% off the cover price. It's quite a bargain! Shipping and handling is just 50¢ per book in the U.S. and 75¢ per book in Canada.* I understand that accepting the 2 free books and gifts places me under no obligation to buy anything. I can always return a shipment and cancel at any time. Even if I never buy another book, the two free books and gifts are mine to keep forever.

110/310 IDN GH6P

| | | |
|---|---|---|
| Name | (PLEASE PRINT) | |
| Address | | Apt. # |
| City | State/Prov. | Zip/Postal Code |

Signature (if under 18, a parent or guardian must sign)

### Mail to the **Reader Service:**
**IN U.S.A.:** P.O. Box 1867, Buffalo, NY 14240-1867
**IN CANADA:** P.O. Box 609, Fort Erie, Ontario L2A 5X3

**Are you a current subscriber to Love Inspired® Suspense books
and want to receive the larger-print edition?
Call 1-800-873-8635 or visit www.ReaderService.com.**

* Terms and prices subject to change without notice. Prices do not include applicable taxes. Sales tax applicable in N.Y. Canadian residents will be charged applicable taxes. Offer not valid in Quebec. This offer is limited to one order per household. Not valid for current subscribers to Love Inspired Suspense larger-print books. All orders subject to credit approval. Credit or debit balances in a customer's account(s) may be offset by any other outstanding balance owed by or to the customer. Please allow 4 to 6 weeks for delivery. Offer available while quantities last.

**Your Privacy**—The Reader Service is committed to protecting your privacy. Our Privacy Policy is available online at www.ReaderService.com or upon request from the Reader Service.

We make a portion of our mailing list available to reputable third parties that offer products we believe may interest you. If you prefer that we not exchange your name with third parties, or if you wish to clarify or modify your communication preferences, please visit us at www.ReaderService.com/consumerschoice or write to us at Reader Service Preference Service, P.O. Box 9062, Buffalo, NY 14240-9062. Include your complete name and address.

LISLP15

# LARGER-PRINT BOOKS!

## GET 2 FREE LARGER-PRINT NOVELS PLUS 2 FREE MYSTERY GIFTS

*Love Inspired®*

### Larger-print novels are now available...

**YES!** Please send me 2 FREE LARGER-PRINT Love Inspired® novels and my 2 FREE mystery gifts (gifts are worth about $10). After receiving them, if I don't wish to receive any more books, I can return the shipping statement marked "cancel." If I don't cancel, I will receive 6 brand-new novels every month and be billed just $5.49 per book in the U.S. or $5.99 per book in Canada. That's a savings of at least 19% off the cover price. It's quite a bargain! Shipping and handling is just 50¢ per book in the U.S. and 75¢ per book in Canada.* I understand that accepting the 2 free books and gifts places me under no obligation to buy anything. I can always return a shipment and cancel at any time. Even if I never buy another book, the two free books and gifts are mine to keep forever.

122/322 IDN GH6D

| | |
|---|---|
| Name | (PLEASE PRINT) |

| | |
|---|---|
| Address | Apt. # |

| | | |
|---|---|---|
| City | State/Prov. | Zip/Postal Code |

Signature (if under 18, a parent or guardian must sign)

### Mail to the **Reader Service:**
**IN U.S.A.:** P.O. Box 1867, Buffalo, NY 14240-1867
**IN CANADA:** P.O. Box 609, Fort Erie, Ontario L2A 5X3

**Are you a current subscriber to Love Inspired® books
and want to receive the larger-print edition?
Call 1-800-873-8635 or visit www.ReaderService.com.**

\* Terms and prices subject to change without notice. Prices do not include applicable taxes. Sales tax applicable in N.Y. Canadian residents will be charged applicable taxes. Offer not valid in Quebec. This offer is limited to one order per household. Not valid to current subscribers to Love Inspired Larger-Print books. All orders subject to credit approval. Credit or debit balances in a customer's account(s) may be offset by any other outstanding balance owed by or to the customer. Please allow 4 to 6 weeks for delivery. Offer available while quantities last.

**Your Privacy**—The Reader Service is committed to protecting your privacy. Our Privacy Policy is available online at www.ReaderService.com or upon request from the Reader Service.

We make a portion of our mailing list available to reputable third parties that offer products we believe may interest you. If you prefer that we not exchange your name with third parties, or if you wish to clarify or modify your communication preferences, please visit us at www.ReaderService.com/consumerschoice or write to us at Reader Service Preference Service, P.O. Box 9062, Buffalo, NY 14240-9062. Include your complete name and address.

LILP15

# REQUEST YOUR FREE BOOKS!
## 2 FREE WHOLESOME ROMANCE NOVELS IN LARGER PRINT
## PLUS 2 FREE MYSTERY GIFTS

### H E A R T W A R M I N G™
*Wholesome, tender romances*

**YES!** Please send me 2 FREE Harlequin® Heartwarming Larger-Print novels and my 2 FREE mystery gifts (gifts worth about $10). After receiving them, if I don't wish to receive any more books, I can return the shipping statement marked "cancel." If I don't cancel, I will receive 4 brand-new larger-print novels every month and be billed just $5.24 per book in the U.S. or $5.99 per book in Canada. That's a savings of at least 19% off the cover price. It's quite a bargain! Shipping and handling is just 50¢ per book in the U.S. and 75¢ per book in Canada.* I understand that accepting the 2 free books and gifts places me under no obligation to buy anything. I can always return a shipment and cancel at any time. Even if I never buy another book, the two free books and gifts are mine to keep forever.

161/361 IDN GHX2

Name _____ (PLEASE PRINT) _____

Address _____ Apt. # _____

City _____ State/Prov. _____ Zip/Postal Code _____

Signature (if under 18, a parent or guardian must sign) _____

### Mail to the **Reader Service**:
**IN U.S.A.:** P.O. Box 1867, Buffalo, NY  14240-1867
**IN CANADA:** P.O. Box 609, Fort Erie, Ontario  L2A 5X3

\* Terms and prices subject to change without notice. Prices do not include applicable taxes. Sales tax applicable in N.Y. Canadian residents will be charged applicable taxes. Offer not valid in Quebec. This offer is limited to one order per household. Not valid for current subscribers to Harlequin Heartwarming larger-print books. All orders subject to credit approval. Credit or debit balances in a customer's account(s) may be offset by any other outstanding balance owed by or to the customer. Please allow 4 to 6 weeks for delivery. Offer available while quantities last.

**Your Privacy**—The Reader Service is committed to protecting your privacy. Our Privacy Policy is available online at www.ReaderService.com or upon request from the Reader Service.

We make a portion of our mailing list available to reputable third parties that offer products we believe may interest you. If you prefer that we not exchange your name with third parties, or if you wish to clarify or modify your communication preferences, please visit us at www.ReaderService.com/consumerchoice or write to us at Reader Service Preference Service, P.O. Box 9062, Buffalo, NY 14240-9062. Include your complete name and address.